CONSEQUENTIAL

A HUMMINGBIRD MURDER MYSTERY

T C PARKER

*For Austrian Spencer -
the best damn editor in the business*

CONTENT WARNINGS

Like its predecessor *To Coventry*, this book is in many ways a dark comedy. And, like *To Coventry*, it touches on some very serious themes and topics about which I care deeply – and about which I, like many of the characters in the story, continue to be quite angry.

It's important I think not to shy away from discussion of these themes and topics, in fiction and elsewhere – but I have no interest in causing any reader undue distress.

Content warnings therefore apply for:

- Torture (primarily off-page)
- Extreme violence (primarily off-page)
- Murder and body disposal
- Blood and gore
- Hallucination
- Drug use and addiction (off-page)

Please let me know via email, as always, if there are any others I should have included.

ONE

GRADY

Hauling corpses up and down the country was exhausting, Grady was discovering. So, when he eventually finished decanting the last of the bodies from their bloodied black refuse sacks onto the living room floor, he allowed himself to rest a moment: to lean back against the bare wall, sink to the ground and close his eyes.

He realised he'd fallen asleep where he squatted only when the gurgling of the body closest to him startled him awake. The noise was terrible, impossible to ignore: ragged and moist, the liquid rasp of a water balloon in a threshing machine. It wasn't the *quality* of the sound that Grady found alarming, though. The body in question had no vocal cords left to speak of, its throat burned to ruin by a complex cocktail of acids Grady couldn't begin to name. What could it do *but* gurgle, in that state?

No. The alarming part, the part that caused Grady to spring up from sitting like a marionette on a wire, was that the body – the body which ought to have been dead, and *long* dead – could be making any sound at all.

Slowly, heart racing but limbs sluggish, Grady crept

towards it – the blue plastic covers he'd slipped on over his John Lobb loafers crunching and rustling with every step.

Its eyes were open. Wide open. Staring at Grady.

It – *he* – was sprawled face-down on the floorboards. Splayed out like a starfish, exactly as Grady had deposited him. But he'd found the strength, somehow, to raise his chin and twist his neck in such a way as to keep Grady in his line of sight.

If he *could* see, that was. Much like the others, he was in an appalling state: veins sliced and skin corroded, the fingers of one hand torn and swollen and the other hand severed roughly from the forearm at the wrist, where only a raw red stump remained. And his eyes had taken as much damage from the acids as his lips and throat – the burst vessels and clouded corneas giving him a zombie-ish appearance complemented by his filthy, shredded clothes.

Grady could take no credit for *those*, obviously. They'd been every bit as filthy, if not quite as shredded, when Grady had found him down on the beach in Brighton: young and strong, the way Grady had needed him, but drunk and pliable, the cold and the cider and the prospect of another night sleeping on a pebble mattress under old tarpaulin more than enough incentive for him to follow Grady to the car and let himself be driven somewhere, anywhere else.

He opened his blistered mouth, and another of the terrible sounds poured out of it – louder this time, like the caw of a crow with its beak in a birdbath.

And Grady realised, dread leaching into his bones, that he was going to have to make him stop.

He crept closer, until his face was barely inches from the man's – its corrosions filling Grady's vision all the way to the edges. Inside their gloves, Grady's fingertips twitched.

Suffocation: it would have to be suffocation. A hand holding shut what remained of the mouth; a forefinger and thumb sealing off what remained of the nostrils until the oxygen no longer flowed and the heart stopped beating.

Could he do it, though? He wasn't sure. It was so... personal. Intimate. He'd have to reach out and *touch* the man, the *body*. And with his own two hands – barely a barrier in place between them.

Grady never *did* have much stomach for physical contact.

Swallowing his fear, and the disgust that came with it, he brought one palm to hover over the suppurating hole in the cawing man's face.

The man's breathing... slowed. Then, as Grady watched, ceased entirely – the lacerated chest neither rising nor falling as it should.

For a full five minutes Grady waited, afraid to move even a muscle. Finally, when it was clear the body had no further breath in it, he broke away. Retreated to the wall, to his earlier spot on the floor and thanked God for the intervention, for sparing Grady the horror of the act.

He stayed there until dawn. Until the beginnings of decomposition rose to meet the blood-and-chemical bouquet the bodies had brought with them and he had to get away.

TWO

SUNNY

In the very large kitchen of a farmhouse in the Forest of Dean, the demon Sunny – immortal, louche and all too easily bored – is repelling the attentions of a pig.

And no ordinary pig. *This* pig, a closer cousin of the regionally nonextant wild boar, stands some four feet when quadrupedal, and measures no fewer than *six* feet from nose to tail: the size, Sunny estimates, of an adolescent polar bear. The fur is coarse and grey, the tusks as proud and curling as a Victorian gentleman's moustaches, and the musk it exudes banishes all other manner of fragrance from the room.

It has, to Sunny's surprise and consternation, taken something of a shine to her.

"He likes the company," the creature's current custodian tells her, needlessly. "We don't get too many visitors out here."

Sunny considers the farmhouse and its location: ten miles from the nearest town, and accessible only through a quarter mile of dense, unpopulated woodland. Then considers the many unseen wards and highly visible security fences that surround the property, installed with the sole intent of holding would-be callers at bay.

"Can't imagine why," she says.

The great pig's keeper laughs, loud and uproarious. "Maybe he just likes *you*. You think about that?"

She looks to the pig, and then to Sunny. Presses a palm to her stomach and laughs again, unable to contain her mirth.

She is, on the face of things, a woman: tall and slender as a willow, her dark skin framed by heavy, pure-white braids that fall almost to her waist. Her skirts are long and colourful, better suited to the Easter Carnival than the contemporary São Paulo neighbourhood from which she's recently departed; there are beads, and feathers, and the possibility of scales below the multitudinous layers of fabric. Her feet are bare, the nails painted emerald and gold; her smile is dazzling. Thus she is, unquestionably, more human-passing than Sunny. Or more human-passing, perhaps, than Sunny's current and default aspect, which has, even Sunny must concede, a bluer hue and greater aggregate of hooves and antlers than is conventional in most variations of the anthropoid form.

Until, that is, one reaches the almost-woman's eyes – which, unlike Sunny's, burn a bright, volcanic red. The red, wholly appropriately, of blood moons and vengeance.

"Anyhow," she says, as her laughter dies away. "What is it you need from us, my friend? The Beast and I would love to hear it."

The Beast in question nuzzles at Sunny's stomach, impatient for attention. It is, Sunny has just this afternoon learned, a native of the Forest: the mythic Beast of Dean, its legend absorbed into the fabric of local folklore even while its very real physical, and indeed olfactory, presence continued to make itself known on occasion to the more adventurous, and thereafter generally rather startled ramblers of Gloucestershire and Avon.

Alandra, the almost-woman – though it's no more her given name than *Sunny* is Sunny's – apparently discovered the Beast on her first day in the Forest, when – drawn by the possibility of a playmate – the animal had sprung at her from a thicket of sweet chestnut saplings, and she was forced to restrain it with a length of rope secreted, for reasons Sunny has yet to fathom, at all times upon her person.

The Beast has kept Alandra company in her rented farmhouse ever since, as docile in her presence as a cocker spaniel, and every bit as excitable. She will, she has already informed Sunny, be heartbroken to leave him behind once when her business in England is concluded and she returns to Brazil.

What *business* this might be Sunny hasn't asked, and Alandra hasn't told, though Sunny is confident she could hazard a guess, given the almost-woman's expertise and interests.

"I was hoping," Sunny begins, "to ask a favour of you."

"Of *course* you were." Alandra laughs again, loud enough now to perturb the Beast, which seeks refuge behind Sunny. "They hear you're in town, and suddenly *everyone* wants a favour. *Uma cara de pau* all of you have, I swear."

"A quid pro quo, then," Sunny says, slipping into Portuguese despite Alandra's *when in Rome* preference for the modern English. "A favour for a favour."

"I'm listening." Alandra clicks her tongue at the Beast, and the pig untangles itself from Sunny; trots away to the pile of blankets that serves as its indoor sleeping area, curls itself into a fleshy ball of tusk and bristle, and closes its eyes. Soon enough, it is snoring.

Sunny raises her voice a fraction, so as to be heard over the snuffling and wheezing. "There is a certain revenant to whom I made a promise, some weeks past. The Lady Godiva, of Cofa's Tree. You may know of her?"

"I've heard something, maybe." Alandra pauses, considering the question. "Medieval lady? Rode a horse somewhere naked and had some asshole stare at her through a window?"

"Something like that." And once again, Sunny thinks with a suppressed sigh, folklore and nursery rhymes fail to communicate anything like *context* to the casual listener.

"And she's dead, this lady?"

"Oh, yes. Long, long dead. A purely spectral phenomenon these days." *Albeit*, Sunny adds to herself, *with a greater capacity than one might expect of a dead woman for inflicting agonising death upon the living.*

"But you promised her something?" There's no incredulity in Alandra's query; no scepticism that the Lady should have elicited such a promise, in spite of her exanimate condition. Merely a desire for clarity.

"I did." Sunny hesitates, considering how best to frame the predicament, and the proposition. "I told her – *assured* her – I would find a way to punish her husband for his past transgressions. To, and here I quote the Lady verbatim, *make him suffer.*"

Delight plays at the corners of Alandra's crimson mouth, as Sunny had hoped it would. *Suffering*, after all, is the almost-woman's stock-in-trade, at least where righteously dispensed.

"And this husband," she asks, "he is also dead?"

Sunny reflects briefly on the life and times of the former

Mr Lady Godiva: Leofric, Earl of Mercia, born somewhere at the junction of the 10th and 11th centuries. "One would hope so," she confirms. "Nevertheless, Godiva is keen to have her vengeance, and I pledged – perhaps rashly, on reflection – that I would make it so."

"You require a necromancer, then?"

"I do," Sunny admits.

I shouldn't require one, *she thinks but doesn't say. Because truth be told, Alandra, I have* one already: *a young man who, despite his youth and inexperience, has more power even than you at his disposal. A young man who might summon and torment a* hundred *Leofrics, were his conscience to permit it.*

Unfortunately for all of us, the boy has... principles.

("No way," Jonas had told her, quite categorically, when Sunny had requested his assistance on the Problem of Leofric. "Absolutely no way. You can't just... raise some old king from the dead so you can torture him, even if he *was* a complete bastard to his wife a thousand years ago. Just... no."

The boy's long, messy fringe of yellow hair had flopped comically about his forehead as his indignation grew, though Sunny had thought better than to mention it in the moment.

"A *complete* bastard," Sunny had concurred. "Thoroughly deserving of punishment, in my estimation. Moreover he is, as you note, dead – traditional ethical frameworks can hardly be applied. *No body, no crime,*" she'd added, in hope that the reference might sway him to her cause. She'd heard him listening often enough to the song in question: he had *some* sympathy for its sentiments, surely?

"It's still a no," he'd said, and wandered away to make coffee in Sunny's newly acquired cold-brew drip tower).

Alandra appears to reflect on the request – or, as is perhaps more likely, to weigh up what she might ask for in return. "I will punish your dead man for you," she says eventually.

"Wonderful," Sunny beams, and waits for the other shoe to drop.

"In return," Alandra continues, "I must ask something of you."

"Would this be something *specific?*"

Sunny assumes it must be. If, however, it is *not*, and Alandra is receptive to alternative suggestions... it may be that Sunny has something to offer her yet. "I am, of course, amenable to any terms you have in mind. But should there *be* no such... specificities: how might you feel about a hamper of Pasteis de Nata as a bargaining chip? I've been availing myself of the rudiments of baking these last months. And while I confess I've yet to put such skills as I've acquired into practice, I'm confident I shall demonstrate an affinity with a pastry brush and egg yolk, as the need arises."

"You wish to trade the dispensation of my fury for a basket of pastries?" Sunny can *hear* the smirk, even as Alandra strives to keep her expression neutral.

"I was rather hoping the dispensation of the fury might be its *own* reward," she says, mildly aggrieved.

"And it is!" Alandra agrees, with a snap of the fingers and an expansive undulation of the arm so archetypically Brazilian Sunny fears for a second that she's apt to be swept up in an embrace. "Or it *would be*, you understand? *Usually*. But today... today, no. Today I have a problem of my own, and *you*, monstrinho – you may be just the remedy. You know I am to return next month to Sampa?"

Sunny shakes her head, and begins to respond, but is

interrupted by a loud, spluttering snort from the corner of the kitchen, where the Beast still sleeps.

Alandra favours the creature with a look of adoration so indulgent it borders on the maternal. "For a week, and only a week. There is a wedding there I must attend. A most beautiful wedding, up in the mountains. The bride is... a client of mine. A very *valuable* client, you know? At least seven years now we have worked together."

Sunny nods, feeling the smallest stirrings of sympathy for the groom – who will at least, she assumes, think twice before straying from the marital bed.

"The trouble," Alandra continues, "is this: I cannot take *that* one back home with me." She waves a hand towards the unconscious Beast in its nest of blankets. It snorts again, and rolls onto its back, smiling beatifically – lost in whatever porcine dreams envelop it. "He must stay here. But leaving him alone, even for only a week... it worries me. He was wild when he found me, yes. But he's become..." She snaps her fingers a second time: three sharp *clicks*, in quick succession. "What's the word I am looking for, the English word?"

"Lazy?" Sunny hazards.

"*Dependent.*" Alandra glares at her, displeased. "Without me here, who knows if he would eat properly, if he would rest?"

Sunny regards from a distance the giant – and very recently feral – hog that was once the scourge of rural England, its muscled hide, and canines sharp enough to puncture diamond. A mixing bowl of water and a half-eaten platter of thick-cut steaks have been placed beside its bedding; a stuffed, already well-chewed toy piglet in a festive waistcoat – intended, the badge it sports declares,

FOR THE WORLD'S BEST BOY – now nestles snugly between the creature's trotters.

"Am I to infer," she asks, "that you wish me to *pet-sit* this animal, in recompense for your services?"

Alandra's smile returns, brighter than ever. "I knew you'd understand."

———

RESIGNED TO HER FATE, Sunny flies in the form of a kestrel from the Forest to the Smoke, and therein to the high-walled garden of her Bloomsbury townhouse – where, shielded from public view, she adopts again the contours of the shape she's come to think of as *herself*.

The back door is unlocked. No thief, she's sure, would last for long against the defensive magicks Jonas, ever mindful of the *cultural value* of the treasures Sunny has amassed across millennia, has persuaded her to employ of late within the house in lieu of an alarm system.

Bipedal now, she pushes the door open and crosses the threshold, ducking low so that her antlers might avoid yet further collision with the doorframe. Passes through the laundry and what was once the scullery, along the draughty hallway and into the living room – where, she hopes, she might collapse into the familiar embrace of her fainting couch and while away the remainder of the evening with a reading from the Book of Kells, or perhaps an episode of *Veep*.

But where instead she finds Jonas and his husband-to-be, straight-backed and hand-in-hand on the couch in question: one boy crying and the other looking up at her expectantly, as if in answer to their prayers.

THREE

SUNNY

Both boys rise from the couch as Sunny enters the room, their joined hands separating so sharply and their smooth cheeks reddening so rapidly she might as well have discovered them *in flagrante* on the Kerman rug.

"Have we abandoned our commitment to *scheduled* visits?" she asks, sweeping past them and ensconcing herself in a vast leather Eileen Gray armchair, newly purloined at Sunny's behest from the private collection of a Stockholm record producer.

"We tried to call," Jonas tells her. Nay, *admonishes* her: as if her refusal to engage with the mobile communications device he and his paramour insisted she acquire signifies some inexcusable moral failing on her part. "You didn't answer."

Though he doesn't look to have been crying – unlike the young man beside him, from whose reddened eyes fresh tears still stream – he is nevertheless quite visibly uneasy: his jaw tightly clenched, and the small creases that manifest only when he's anxious sprung up like complex lacework across the surface of his forehead.

Something is wrong, Sunny deduces.

"We need your help," the other boy, Dan, says, his Queen's English choked with saltwater and mucus – though help with *what*, Sunny can't imagine. She's been gone scarcely a day, and both boys seemed in fine fettle before her departure: Jonas obsessing happily over the latest chapter of his thesis – the subject of which continues to elude her, but may have something to do with anthropology, or sociology, or possibly some other more *social* of the sciences – and Dan describing with mounting excitement and quite unnecessary specificity the details of a farming-themed computer game he and his software company are in the process of designing. Sheep are involved, in some capacity. Cattle feed, likewise, and humorously anthropomorphic potatoes.

Both boys moreover appeared – to Sunny's eye – quite unnaturally happy *with one another*, the glow of their recent engagement and accompanying holiday to Miami yet to entirely recede even as the wedding day itself approaches. Invites have been written and gift registry alerts disseminated as far afield as Seoul, whence Dan's Korean grandparents are domiciled, and Lima, last known location of Jonas' dissolute brother Louis. Fiona, Jonas' step-mother, has been commissioned to give a reading at the ceremony, one punctuated no doubt with as many allusions to lunar goddesses and ancestral veneration as the old witch can squeeze into a seven-minute time slot.

All, in short, had been well.

"My help?" Sunny's curiosity outweighs (for now) her desire to remind Jonas of his reluctance to provide a simi-lar help to *her*, where *his* was so recently solicited – though the urge to do so remains, screaming to be heard on the peripheries of her cognisance. She will, she promises herself, find an appropriate moment to drop into the conversation some pithy but scalding reference to his hypocrisy; just as soon as Dan's tears and the overarching strangeness of this sitting room tableau have been explained away.

"Someone we know has gone missing," Jonas says, the manner of his speech uncharacteristically taciturn. "A friend. We thought you might be able to help us find him. You know... track him down."

He looks to his betrothed for confirmation. Reaches out tentatively and retrieves his hand, coiling Dan's fingers around his own and squeezing gently.

"Track him down?" Sunny repeats, as surprised by the framing of the question as by the request itself. "I believe you have me mistaken for a bounty hunter. Perhaps a scent hound of some description."

"I know you could do it," Jonas insists. "*You* know you could do it, if you wanted to. You move fast, you can look like basically anything you want... and you've got that *thing*, haven't you? That hypnosis thing, where people tell you stuff, even if they don't want to. Confess things to you, pass on secrets. *We* can't do that."

Ah: the *thrall*. Of *course*, the thrall. She curses the day she let the boy in on the knowledge of that particular capacity for coercion. Even the most bovine of dalcops would have viewed with suspicion the naif's interest he expressed at the time in the art and its applications.

He has, she suspects now, been pondering ever since how it might best be harnessed in the spirit of *doing good*.

"I'm afraid I'm busy." She stretches her legs across the chair's sculptured armrest and flexes all four of her toes towards him for emphasis. "Just prodigiously busy, right at this moment."

Jonas releases his grip on his inamorato, shifting into

what she's come to think of as his *debating society* posture, scratching at his chin and rubbing a palm against the back of his neck as he formulates a riposte, the mot juste required to gather Sunny to the side of righteousness. To induce her, after all, to *help*.

It's Dan who speaks first, however. Quietly and tearfully, yes. But not *thoughtlessly*. The boy, she recognises later if not in the moment of his speaking, is careful in spite of his sincerely felt upset to seed in his petition *just enough* mystery to awaken her interest. Enough, and *just* enough of the possibility of a puzzle to be solved, a problematic knot to be untangled, that she, ever inquisitive, has no choice but to listen.

———

THE MISSING *FRIEND*, it transpires, is not *only* a friend, but Dan's former lover: the man with whom he lived during his studies at Oxford and for two years thereafter, immediately prior to the formation of the current Dan/Jonas partnership. While subtext has never been Sunny's forte, and the all-too-human nuances of unspoken and paralinguistic communication have long struck her as something of a blind alley for all involved, it seems to her there may be more emotional weight and complexity yet to the relationship between all three players than has been explicitly disclosed: that the missing boy may have been not only Dan's *first* love but his *only* love before Jonas emerged from the wings, and that the fact of this remains a sore point for the latter couplet. A patch of rough and needle-strewn terrain in the otherwise smooth and gently undulating unfolding of their soon-to-be marital bliss.

Is *this*, she wonders, why one boy now stands before her

weeping, and the other so riddled with tension she can very nearly feel it vibrating along his sinews?

Could it be that the two of them were *arguing* in the moments before her arrival – and in her living room, no less?

The former lover's name, she learns, is Sean Keane. And he is, by Dan's own admission, in many respects exactly the kind of man one might expect to disappear unannounced in the dead of night, only to *reappear* hours or days hence.

"He drinks a lot," is how Dan puts it. "Drinks to *get* drunk – on his own, not just when he's out. And sometimes he'll... go wandering. Get it into his head that he needs to *be* somewhere, right then – Margate or, I don't know, the Louvre – and just... take himself off there. Without telling anyone."

"The smack probably doesn't help," Jonas adds, with more bitterness than his ordinarily sweet disposition would usually allow. "Who's going to remember where they're supposed to be tomorrow afternoon with that much gear in their system?"

Dan shakes his head. Not angry at the interjection, Sunny infers, but hurt. *Disappointed.*

"He's not an *addict*," he tells Sunny of the absent Keane – apologetically, as if the man were predisposed not to the delectations of the poppy but to bursting into song around the dinner table after one glass too many of the House Bordeaux. "He doesn't inject, nothing like that. He just... isn't always good at *dealing* with things, you know? At being in the world, without something holding him up or levelling him out."

Sunny takes note of, but passes no comment upon, the eye-roll Jonas directs to the ceiling at this supplementary detail.

Keane also conducts, it seems – at least by Dan's account – something of a double life.

"He wasn't out. Isn't. To his family, I mean. Or the people he works with – *when* he works, anyway. He's not been brilliant at keeping jobs when he's had them, historically. And I *know* nobody would care that he's gay, and I think even *Sean* knows it deep down, but still..."

"His parents would," Jonas says, quietly – placing a hand, silently apologetic, in the small of Dan's back.

Dan leans into it. And thus, Sunny thinks, the earlier transgression is forgiven. For now, anyway. "Yes," he agrees, "they probably would, wouldn't they? They're Catholic," he tells Sunny. "*Very* Catholic. Mass every day, portraits of the Virgin Mary on the walls, rosaries in the car, the whole business."

To Sunny, for whom Constantine's First Council of Nicaea represented less a defining moment of empyrean revelation and more a means of bringing the warring tribes of Alexandria to heel, the contemporary trappings of the faith are at best an exercise in self-branding. But this feels, once again, not quite the time to mention it.

"Plus, the dad...," Jonas begins, then falters, walking now on eggshells in his descriptions of the missing Sean Keane and his family, if solely for Dan's benefit. "He's kind of a gangster. Irish mafia."

"Don't exaggerate." Dan's tone and expression are only lightly chiding. "The man runs a waste disposal business. Not everything he does may be strictly kosher, and he's got a temper, but he's not Al Capone."

Sunny wonders whether the boy has ever heard of the Gambinos or the Genoveses. Or if, indeed, he's ever watched *The Sopranos*.

"You believe the father's business dealings are responsible for the younger Keane's vanishing?" Sunny asks, eager to keep the conversation progressing along this more tantalising route. The amorous entanglements of youth are as quotidian now as they ever were – but the introduction of an organised criminal element lends the tale of the evanescing libertine a very welcome spice.

"No." Dan shakes his head – though Jonas, she observes, remains silently sceptical. "I mean... maybe. But I don't think so. His mum was the one who called to tell me he was gone. She's in Dublin, but they talk a lot. A few times a week at least. He never forgets to call her, even when he's, you know... on one of his benders. They're close. Really close. Or as close as you can be to someone when you're lying to them about more or less your entire life and identity."

I see, Sunny thinks – the reason for the dissolution of that *particular* romance suddenly apparent, even to her. Opium and aqua vitae were par for the course, it seems, but the allegorical closet was a bridge too far.

"Nobody's heard from him in a fortnight," Dan continues. "Nobody. Not his mum, not his housemate, no-one. It's... very unusual."

"He hasn't been calling *Dan*, either," says Jonas, the effort of keeping his composure, his equilibrium, evidently costing him dearly. "Or texting him. Which apparently is a thing Sean does a lot, but that *I* just found out about today."

"I'm sorry." Dan reaches for Jonas, his voice scarcely a whisper. For another kind of onlooker, Sunny thinks, the intimacy of the moment, the involuntary voyeurism of it might be freighted with awkwardness; a third-wheel discomfort. The sensation perhaps that one ought to be elsewhere, with one's eyes averted.

She, fortunately, is encumbered with no such anxieties.

"To sum up, then," she says, she says, her voice assuming an Italian American inflection. "The Keane boy is missing, possibly abducted by, if you will, *the mob* – and you wish me to help you find him. You don't ask with respect. You don't *offer* help, when I have needed it. I don't remember the last time you invited me to your apartment for a slice of Battenberg, even though I have more than once let *myself* in to water your cheese-plants. You don't even think to call me *mighty* or *exalted*, in recognition of my powers. Instead you come into my house on the day I had planned to watch television and douse myself with scented oils in a bath of bubbles, and you ask me to do detective work. For no money whatsoever."

Jonas turns to Dan. "I *told* you we shouldn't have let her watch *The Godfather*."

"It was that or *Alien*, and *then* where would we be?"

"Look." Jonas returns his attention to Sunny. "I know it's a big ask. I know you've... got a lot on." To his credit, the boy maintains a neutral expression even as he delivers this obvious lie. "But you can see how upset he is," he indicates Dan with a nod of the head, "and we'd really, really appreciate you helping us get to the bottom of this. We'd be...," he winces, "... in your debt. You can, you know... call upon us to do a service for you. Or something."

"Please," Dan says.

Sunny chews over their plea. It *does* appeal to her, this mystery, with its troubled-but-degenerate protagonist and its suggestion of hoodlum mystique. And she *has*, it's true, developed a taste for sleuthing, just lately.

But nothing, as Alandra so recently declaimed, is without a price.

And the price here must be steep enough to justify the toil.

"What *kind* of service?" she asks.

"Anything you want," Jonas says. Then, perhaps realising the folly of such a covenant: "Cake. We'll bring you cake. A *proper* cake: home-made, iced, everything."

She considers this. "And what *kind* of cake, precisely?"

FOUR

GRADY

The old man weighed practically nothing anymore, and he'd been folded up like a concertina in an upright suitcase, but Grady hadn't counted on the stairs – on having to drag him up six urine-smelling flights in the almost-dark, with only the spluttering fluorescence of a defective bulb to light his way.

He should've anticipated it. The lifts were always out of action in these council blocks, weren't they? Nothing ever worked, and nobody ever came to fix what was broken. If your flat was on the seventh floor, you *walked* there, and if you couldn't walk, you crawled on your belly or you stayed inside and hoped someone out there cared enough to bring you what you needed to survive.

Though that was what you got, Grady supposed, when you made the choice to live in squalor. And at least he could be sure there was no real surveillance in a place like this. No working cameras mounted on the walls to catch him in the act.

Breathless and sweating under the baseball cap that hid his face and the gloves that smothered his fingers, he lugged the suitcase behind him up the final set of steps, turned left into a narrow communal hallway that reeked of stale beer and cannabis smoke and navigated past a dozen other door numbers before he got to 619. The old man's flat.

With the old man's key – a stained Yale thing on a Rooster of Barcelos key ring, a memento Grady assumed from some long-ago package holiday to Madeira or the Algarve – he let himself in, pulling the suitcase after him, and locked the door.

Inside, even with the lights on, the flat was as sad and dingy as he remembered it: the walls bare, painted a shade of mint that should have died with the '70s, and the living room-kitchen so sparsely furnished it could've been a MoMA installation or an especially bleak IKEA showroom. A battered leather chair patched with duct tape squatted opposite a small television set in a wooden cabinet; beside the chair stood a side-table, supporting a remote control and a plastic ashtray – stolen, probably, from a pub – that threatened to overflow with roll-up cigarette butts and piles of dead grey ash.

There were no books, no computers, no pens or pencils; no instruments to play or music to listen to. Nothing to suggest the old man ever did much more than smoke and watch TV, and – if the still-pungent after-scent of body odour in the air was anything to go by – sweat with the intensity of a marathon runner into the armpits of his charity-shop shirts.

Really, he'd hardly existed at all.

On the threadbare carpet of the living room area, Grady laid the suitcase flat and unfastened it, peeling back the lid to reveal the old man's body within: no longer naked, as he had been, but still obviously emaciated, his bony kneecaps tenting the polyester of his trousers and his hollowed-out eye-sockets giving him the look of a forlorn Grim Reaper who'd misplaced his scythe. Even after weeks of malnutrition, of almost-starvation, he'd kept much of his hair, though Grady noticed that a few grey clumps had fallen away from the scalp here and there. Still: you couldn't help but marvel at the resilience of the man, of the biological systems that had held him together. Neither Grady's spirit nor his body, he was sure, would have clung on half as long or half as tightly in the old man's place.

He hooked his arms around the old man's triceps and hauled him semi-upright, then backwards, pulling him onto the chair and arranging him into a recreation of what Grady imagined he must have looked like in life: legs splayed, one hand resting on the side-table, slumped head facing the television. It wasn't quite perfect: the beginnings of rigor mortis had already set the body's forearms at a faintly unnatural angle, and the lollipop-head kept succumbing to gravity and falling onto the old man's pigeon chest no matter *how* Grady positioned it. But it was good enough. It would do.

Satisfied, Grady picked up the remote control and turned on the television. Opened the old man's curled and stiffening fingers and placed the remote control between them.

To the casual observer – perhaps even to the police officers who would eventually kick in the door and find the body when the smell became so unbearable not even *these* neighbours could ignore it, if not to the coroner who examined him afterwards – it might seem as if he'd died right there in his armchair, in front of the television. From a heart attack, maybe. A stroke. Or some other of the ravages of poverty and malnutrition.

The scene set, Grady moved on to the kitchenette. There was nothing much to worry about in the fridge: a pint of curdled milk; a loaf of bread, mouldy despite the cold; a block of hardened cheese, ridden with white spots; a bunch of grapes that had seen better days. He poured the milk down the sink; threw the bottle, the bread, the cheese and the grapes into the suitcase to take away with him.

There were a few more things than he'd anticipated in the cupboards, though all of them food bank staples: cans of beans and tinned spaghetti, an opened pack of Bourbon biscuits, a box of high-fibre cereal flakes. These too he placed in the suitcase, going item by item through each cupboard until the shelves were bare.

Until all that was left in the flat was Grady and his suitcase, and a television telling stories to an empty room, and an old man who'd starved to death between the cushions of his armchair.

FIVE

SUNNY

Sean Keane's current residence is a shared house in an unlovely enclave northwest of the city, nestled in close proximity to both the grey concrete cube of the Brent Cross shopping centre and the polluted ouroboros of the North Circular: a road so confoundingly labyrinthine in construction it elicits in Sunny a nostalgia for the sacbeob of Chichen Itza.

She flies there, of course – this time as a pigeon, her preferred form in the skies above England's urban sprawl. Comes to land in a deserted alleyway but a moment's walk from her destination and reconfigures herself again – becoming now a human woman, devoid any trace of hoof and antler. In human guise, she is unremarkable: chronologically somewhere in the lower reaches of her fourth decade, of middling height and build and indeterminately Mediterranean appearance – or Middle Eastern, or perhaps Latine. She is clothed head to toe in denim, cotton and the kind of dark blue duffel coat that calls to mind an amiable cartoon bear on a railway platform. Whomsoever opens the door chez Keane, she thinks, they will find her, at least at first, the very model of harmless approachability.

In fact, the boy who answers her unobtrusive press of the house's doorbell is so garrulously cordial, so *friendly* that she might have adopted the slime and clitellum of a Mongolian Death Worm and still have found herself invited in for coffee. He's slim, dark-eyed and youthfully beautiful, wrapped in a flannel dressing gown he wears like a smoking jacket. His name, he tells her as she follows him through to the kitchen, is Amir, and although he works nights – *just bar work, darling; nothing glamorous* – she shouldn't worry about having roused him from sleep, because he needed to be up anyway, lest he waste the day in bed.

Dan has called ahead to give notice of her arrival, and more importantly to apprise Amir-the-housemate, in the broadest possible terms, of the reason for her visit: that she, like Dan, is concerned for the absent Sean's welfare, and has vouchsafed therefore to investigate, beginning by speaking directly to those who know Sean best. Quite what this must make her from Amir's perspective, Sunny cannot fathom. Does he think her a paid gumshoe, hot on the trail – a Philip Marlowe of the Northern Line, and Dan her butter-and-egg man, bankrolling the chase from the shadows? Perhaps an off-duty officer of Scotland Yard, providing more specialist support as her shift patterns allow? Or simply an overzealous amateur with time to kill, a budget Lord Wimsey in toggle-and-rope?

"I'm *so* glad someone's taking it seriously," Amir says, slipping a pod into the coffee machine. "Sean going off like this, I mean. I've been worried sick."

Sunny seats herself at the stripped pine table and takes a moment to acquaint herself with the space around her, and with any Clues she might discover therein. The room is small but feels larger, its unifying aesthetic Japanese-minimalist, all light shades and endlessly signifying emptiness. This is Amir's handiwork, she presumes – Sean, if she's to believe the descriptions with which Dan and especially *Jonas* have furnished her, is more inclined to self-destruction than wabi-sabi. "I understand he does so, though, on occasion? *Goes off* unannounced?"

Amir sets a plain stoneware mug below the coffee dispenser and activates the machine, which slurps and guzzles noisomely, disrupting the cultivated serenity of their surrounds. "Well, *yes*. But not like *this*. Not for this long. It's been weeks, darling – *weeks*. He's never done *this* before, even when he's..." The boy grasps an invisible bottle by its neck and makes a mummer's show of glugging from it.

"And what of the opium?" Sunny asks. "Might that not account for his absence? Might he simply be lost in a laudanum haze, beyond the bounds of the city?"

Dan may have dismissed the possibility, but this strikes her as the most likely explanation for Keane's disappearance. Are not young men inclined towards the pipe, and latterly the aluminium foil, inclined to roam the world untethered? She herself can scarcely count the number of retroactively anointed prophets she's known to have gone wandering the desert for forty days or more after an evening in the floral embrace of the poppy.

"Oh my days, what are you *like*!" Amir slaps a palm to his cheek; lets his eyes widen and his jaw slacken in a parody of shock. ""*A laudanum haze*"? Who *says* that?" When Sunny only shrugs – who is she, after all, to know what she is or isn't *like*? – he continues. "Listen. I'm not stupid. I know the kind of stuff that Sean gets into. I can *smell* it coming out of his bedroom some nights. But he isn't what you'd call a *party boy*, if you know what I mean. He drinks, and does whatever else, but he's not out dancing his tits off or getting fisted in a darkroom. From what *I* can tell, he just stays in and watches films and listens to music until he passes out. And when he *does* go out, when he *stays* out, it's never for more than a day or two. I might not know where he goes, but he always comes back again. Always."

He always comes back. Wasn't that what Dan had said too, more or less?

"You believe something more infelicitous to have befallen him?" she inquires, when Amir has detached the now-full coffee cup from the monstrous machine and brought it to rest on the table.

The boy's finely plucked eyebrows rise as he parses the meaning from the question. "I almost don't want to say it, I hate to even *think* it... but I think I do, yeah. For him to be gone for this long, and not even his *mum* to know where he is... It's got to be something bad, hasn't it?"

Here, at the mention of the mother, Sunny spies a conversational opening: an opportunity to plumb the depths of Amir's knowledge of the Keane family and its criminal empire-building. "That being so," she begins, "might the father's line of work be a factor? If Sean has indeed been... shall we say *abducted*, or otherwise spirited away: would not one of *Mr* Keane's business associates, or indeed his business *rivals* be our logical suspects?"

Amir blinks, rapidly, by way of a response. "I don't know anything about that," he says stiffly, the veneer of gossipy cabaret artist he'd worn previously falling momentarily away to reveal the frightened and altogether more *formal* former public schoolboy beneath. "Sean only ever talked about his mum, not the rest of his family. I've never met them, and none of them have ever been over here to see him. And from what I *do* know of his dad, what I've *heard* about him... I'd much rather keep it that way, if you don't mind. I don't really fancy waking up to a horse's head on the pillow next to me."

Sunny recognises the reference immediately, and the recognition delights her. "What is it exactly you've heard of him? Of his... business model?"

"Nothing I want to talk about. Nothing I'm *going* to talk about." Amir's face, previously so open, is suddenly a Wall of Jericho: sealed-off, and utterly impassable. Sunny considers employing a little of the thrall, to encourage the boy to set aside his worries and share whatever it is he knows of the senior Keane's dealings – until, quite unexpectedly, he adds: "It's not the *dad* you should be looking at, anyway. It's the boyfriend."

"The boyfriend?"

It must, she thinks, be *Sean's* boyfriend to whom Amir refers. And yet, Dan had mentioned no such lover, despite the regular contact it seemed he and Keane maintained in the years following their separation. Despite the many, many phone calls exchanged between them, about which Jonas had appeared so thoroughly aggrieved.

Curious.

"I haven't met *him*, either," Amir says, still guarded. "Sean wouldn't even tell me his name. He's been a real secret squirrel about the whole thing. My guess is the guy's closeted, and he's got a wife or girlfriend waiting for him at home. That, or he's one of those cabinet ministers who goes cruising in the showers at the gym and thinks nobody recognises him from *Question Time*."

With such men, and indeed such women, Sunny is similarly familiar. The assignations may take place now across the saunas and shower rooms of Soho and not the battlefields of Alesia or the royal bedchambers at Hampton Court Palace, but the underlying sentiment remains the same.

"How, then," she asks, "can you be certain he exists, this boyfriend?"

"Trust me, darling." Sunny's interest now diverted away from the racketeering antics of the elder Keane, Amir relaxes back into his earlier, more queenly persona. "He exists. I don't know how much disposable income Sean's *parents* have tucked away offshore, but I've seen some of that boy's bank statements and I guarantee you, he couldn't afford to keep sending *himself* the gifts we've had delivered here the last few months. We're talking boxes from Tiffany, parcels from Harrods, flowers from McQueens... some really gorgeous stuff, way out of *my* price range, let alone his. No, our Sean's got himself a sugar daddy. And a good one, too – one who's good *for him*, I mean. He might be sneaking off into his room and whispering into his phone more than he used to, but he's been happier since it started, definitely. More... smiley. Not quite *chatty*, this is still Sean we're talking about, but happier, for sure. I don't exactly keep track of his units, but I *think* he's been drinking less as well. And calming down, with the..."

In lieu of completing the sentence, Amir bends his head and sniffs, sucking narcotic fumes from an imaginary straw.

Sunny processes this new, perhaps pivotal morsel of data. Is it possible Sean Keane has not, in fact, vanished at all, but is merely in hiding somewhere with his clandestine-but-magnanimous admirer, far from public and maternal reach?

Before she can put this to Amir, however, the boy's dressing gown explodes into song: an early Dolly Parton number, unless Sunny is much mistaken. He frowns; retrieves a large, glitter-encrusted mobile phone from the pocket of the robe and stares at the screen, as if perplexed that anyone should have thought to call it.

"Hello?" he says into the device, when eventually he accedes to the bluegrass demands of its ring. His frown deepens as whomever has placed the call responds. Then, to Sunny's surprises, he hands her the phone.

"It's for you," he tells her, lightly disgruntled, and utterly nonplussed.

Sunny, no less surprised than he, utters a greeting of her own into the handset.

"Oh, good," a familiar voice replies in the old tongue: the language native to Sunny's homeland. "Your friend Jonas said I'd find you on this number. Please do give my apologies to the young man I just spoke to, I think I may have startled him."

And thus, the peculiar phone call begins to make some modicum of sense. None of Sunny's kind, not even those who fancy themselves assimilated, have ever entirely got to grips with the shifting and oh-so-contingent nuances of human etiquette.

"What is it you want, Bunny?" she answers – in English, so as to avoid further startling Amir.

"There's been a murder, up in Birmingham," the voice says. "Several of them, actually. I thought they might be up your street, after... you know. Last time."

Last time, Sunny thinks, is doing an awful lot of heavy lifting in this instance: coyly alluding as it does to the behind-the-scenes participation of her mystery caller in the recent blood-drenched extermination of no fewer than a dozen men in the West Midlands area. And to Sunny's Poirot-like role in unravelling whodunnit thereafter.

Bunny, like Sunny, is bound while on earth by the ancient, arcane – and often, to Sunny's mind, decidedly inconvenient – laws of their own land, which preclude their kind from directly harming any human. *Indirect* harms, however, have proven more permissible, and for this Sunny – who has found in her time myriad ways to circumvent the prohibition – is thankful. Until but a month ago, she'd thought sweet-faced and softly spoken Bunny more Pharisaical than she in her dedication to preserving and protecting human life, whatever its value. Not to say sanctimonious.

Fortunately, she was wrong, her assumption fallacious. And Bunny more brutal and more unscrupulous than she could ever have imagined.

Sunny has come to regard her since in an entirely more positive light.

"It's terribly gruesome," Bunny adds, as if to further awaken Sunny's investigative antennae. "Severed limbs absolutely *everywhere*."

And oh, the offer is tempting.

Nevertheless: "I'm *out on a case*, Bunny," she says. "A *different* case. I have no time for severed limbs just at present."

Amir, attending shamelessly to Sunny's every word, clamps a hand to his mouth in horror.

"Don't tell me you're not curious," Bunny persists. "And it's not as if you have to stay long. Why not just pop up for an hour or two this afternoon and I can fill you in? I *may* have managed to lay my hands on the case files."

It's so tempting. So terribly, terribly tempting. Though Jonas and Dan, Sunny is sure, will look less than kindly on her abandoning her search for Sean Keane just as it's begun, even if only for an afternoon.

As if tracing the flight path of Sunny's thoughts from afar, Bunny plays her ace. "Go *on*," she says. "There are photographs, too. *Crime scene* photographs. Dreadfully grisly stuff – I should think they might shock even *you*."

SIX

SUNNY

The most effective means of avoiding Jonas and Dan's opprobrium vis-a-vis her impromptu visit to the Midlands, it occurs to Sunny, is to simply not tell them she'll be going.

She will however grant Jonas one concession, which she's certain would please him, were he ever to learn of it: she will recover – whence it was last abandoned – the mobile phone he gave her, and she will carry it with her, on her person, all the way to Bunny's Warwickshire retreat.

She does both boys the further courtesy, moreover, of leaving her own telephone number with Amir, lest he wish to contact her directly. Though it is, she will admit, a disappointment to have no business card that she might slip into his hand as she bids him farewell – to have, instead, to manually input the number into *his* phone with an index finger, digit by painstaking digit, as no Sam Spade or Lew Archer ever would.

Encumbered by the device, her capacity for unaided flight constrained by its rebarbative weight, she has no choice but to drive up to Bunny from Bloomsbury: the necessarily *public* dimension of public transport rendering buses, trains and taxicabs no kind of option at all.

She keeps in London, for such eventualities as these, a 1952 Morgan Plus-4 convertible, canary yellow and upholstered in the softest leathers – not so redolent of a horse and carriage as the Abingdon she piloted across England in the earliest days of the automobile, but more comfortable and more aesthetically pleasing by far than the tractor-like four-wheel drives so favoured by the moneyed Britons of the present. Sunny, she must herself acknowledge, is an appalling driver, perennially astonished by the presence of other vehicles and pedestrians on the road. It's testament only to the great infrequency with which she drives – and also she suspects to the wide berth generally afforded those who navigate the capital behind the wheel of a vintage sports car in canary yellow - that she's yet to cause a collision.

Perhaps because of the generous pockets of space that surround her no matter which lane of the motorway she occupies, her journey to the Midlands is both quick and smooth; its soundtrack – a medley of science fiction-themed folk songs performed over electronic beats that Jonas once foisted upon her – a welcome change at least from the ambient urban cacophonies that accompany her winged flights.

Bunny's current abode, she sees as she guides the Morgan along the unnecessarily winding driveway towards it, looks much as it did on her last sojourn to the country-side: like the manor house of a minor Hanoverian aristocrat, latterly repurposed as the vicarage of a well-respected local rector. Sunny would not be surprised in the slightest to learn that it entertained in its pre-Bunny years more than its fair share of murder-mystery theme parties and middle-management corporate retreats.

In anticipation of her arrival, Sunny's host waits to greet her at the door. Bunny too is the same as ever she was: rosy-cheeked and ringleted, the formless beige of her linen tunic a nod to the fashions of the Ptolemaic period for which she evinces such enduring affection.

"I can only hope," Sunny says in the old tongue, as she steps free of the Morgan, "that these crime reports of yours are worth my while. Not all of us are creatures of leisure."

Bunny shrugs off the barb. "You won't be disappointed," she tells Sunny, and leads her inside.

———

THE INTERIOR of the manor house is likewise unchanged: the ragtag collection of ages-old furniture and Ancient Near East trinkets Bunny has inserted into each room – with all the panache of an amateur rôtisseur stuffing a Christmas turkey – still amount to an unprepossessingly parochial whole, despite the prodigious sums any one item would doubtless command, were it to fetch up at Sotheby's or Bonhams.

At least, Sunny notes on entering the dining hall, Bunny has done her the kindness of laying out the crime scene photographs for her perusal: the snapshots posed side-by-side in a single snaking line along the wake table, like tiles upended in an especially gruesome game of dominoes.

"And from whom did you acquire these?" she asks, before allowing herself to study any of the images too closely.

"I did *say* you ought not to ask me," Bunny begins – and then relents. "But fine. If we must. I happen to know someone involved with the case. A police officer. A very *senior* police officer, who shall for our purposes remain nameless. We got chatting one evening, after I'd read about what happened in the paper, and he mentioned he'd been given oversight of the investigation."

A fellow thespian, no doubt, Sunny thinks. *Or perhaps a set-designer.*

Much of Bunny's ample free time of late has been spent bringing turgid life to *Timon of Athens* and *The Merry Wives of Windsor* in the company of the Midgrove Shakespeare Society, a local amateur dramatics association of apparently estimable repute. At least one of its members, Sunny knows, has dabbled in necromancy under Bunny's influence, unwittingly setting in motion the Godiva calamity of the previous month. Thus, the presence within the group of a high-ranking detective with loose lips and a disregard for protocol seems positively prosaic by comparison. Although it may well be that Bunny has deployed a little of the thrall upon him too, the better to encourage the man to part with the photographs now spread before them on the table.

"Talk me through them." Sunny indicates the image nearest to her: a bird's-eye view of what appears to be a tangled smorgasbord of severed human limbs, some pale pink and some brown, all crusted with ichor. "Set the scene for me."

She allows herself a smile at the dramaturgical pun. Bunny does not reciprocate.

"They were five," she tells Sunny sombrely, as if intoning the funeral rites over the bodies of the recently dismembered. "Five men, fit and strong as oxen. Found, in the state you see, in an empty flat on the ground floor of an apartment building in the Jewellery Quarter of Birmingham city centre – the Beormingas territory, as once it was. Some whole and others quartered, hence the... appendages. All of them disfigured: some with blades, some with wire, some with a pellet-like ballistic material not unlike a hollow-point bullet. One man appears to have swallowed sulphuric acid; to have been *doused* in, about the head and neck. Features virtually burned away. But none, curiously, seem to have expired through quite the same means. You'll notice when you read the coroner's report that each suffered a different cause of death. Had they not been found together, and not been so obviously *placed* together, one would be forgiven for assuming they were the victims of five entirely disparate assailants."

Sunny takes in the photographs, frame by forensically catalogued frame: the apostemating wounds, the ostentatious desecrations. And yes: on closer inspection, and accounting for the separation of limb from trunk in some instances, she does indeed count five discrete cadavers, recumbent on a bare wood floor.

"Have your policeman friend and his underlings yet identified who they were and whence they came?" she asks. "One assumes they possessed other attributes in life beyond their propensity to bleed. Names, for example."

Bunny indicates a small mound of manila folders, piled unobtrusively beside the furthest-away of the photos. "All the salient details are there. I thought you might prefer to peruse them for yourself before you and I discuss them. You being such a lone wolf maverick, in matters of detection," she adds – with surprising tartness, for Bunny.

Sunny bestows upon her the sweetest of grins. "Still smarting from the Godiva affair, I see."

Inasmuch as her cherub's face will permit her to do so, Bunny scowls. "I believe I'm going to go and rustle us up some lunch," she says, stiffly. "Will you read the files while I cook?"

"For you, Bunny?" Sunny lays a hand across that area of her chest under which a human woman's heart would ordinarily beat, radiating earnest solemnity. "Anything."

———

AND READ the files she does, even as the fennel and harissa scents of Bunny's overspiced merguez tagine drift into the dining hall from the kitchen.

Only two of the five men, she sees, remain unidentified, though they share with the named victims commonalities of age and stature. As Bunny suggested, each victim is young, aged somewhere between nineteen and thirty, and all – despite variations in height, ethnicity and the quantity of body art exhibited across the canvas of their maimed flesh – would in life have been physically imposing, if not outright hulking. They are heavyweights and welterweights, to a man.

The first named victim, Enzo Rodriguez, was twenty-six. Trained originally as a painter and decorator, he had been out of work for several years prior to his murder and, according to statements given to the police by his mother and sister, had been sleeping rough since the previous July: initially in a tent on beaches in and around his hometown of Bournemouth, and latterly on the streets of Southampton.

He had never, to his family's knowledge, taken so much as a day trip to Birmingham.

The technical cause of Rodriguez' death was recorded as traumatic brain injury: subdural haematoma, likely precipitated by one of the several blows inflicted on his skull in the final hours of his life by means of an unknown but heavy-duty weapon. *This* injury however seems to Sunny rather less significant than the many others rained down upon him: the cracked ribs, the deep scratches and, most especially, the cleaving of both arm and leg from torso on the left side of the body, as if by the action of a guillotine or an unusually large meat slicer.

The second named man, Grayson Kohn, suffered similarly though not identically in the run-up to his expiration. A Mancunian biochemistry graduate with a history of depression, anxiety and self-medication via alcohol abuse, he too had experienced a recent bout of homelessness following his release from a local mental health unit: graduating from couch-surfing with friends in Bury, Rochdale and Rawtenstall to sheltering in doorways in the high streets of Wigan and Bolton before disappearing altogether, to the concern of the few of his relatives who noticed his absence.

His body, like Rodriguez', had been butchered: the hands hacked away at the wrists, accelerating the blood loss that ultimately killed him, and one leg roughly amputated above the knee. Stranger than this though were the markings on his face and chest, a half a dozen overlapping lattices of scabbed and ragged cuts: deep-tissue lacerations of such chequerboard-like appearance that the man might have charged full-frontal into a wall made entirely of cheese wire in the moments preceding his exsanguination.

Both he and Rodriguez, however, might have counted themselves lucky to have escaped the fate of the third and final identified victim, Daniel Kovacs – a former factory worker and one-time Muay Thai fighter from Brighton, discovered among the wreckage of the bodies with all four of his limbs still intact but his lips, his tongue, the back of his throat and one of his eyes eaten away by a chemical agent that reads, to Sunny, as structurally akin to some of the more unpleasant of the twentieth century's mustard gases. His dying in particular, she suspects, would have been long and lingering; he would have suffered, perhaps more acutely than any of the rest.

He, like Kohn and Rodriguez, had no fixed address at the time of his death. And, like them, few remaining friends and relatives to mourn his passing.

Itinerants, then, Sunny thinks, slipping back with ease into her homicide detective's metaphorical fedora. *Whoever our killer may be, he's targeting homeless men. Stealing them from the very streets onto which penury has forced them.*

But not vulnerable *homeless men. Not the old or addled or physically weak – the young and the strong. Prime physical specimens: men who might have been athletes, but for their destitution.*

Which tells us what?

That these men weren't quarry, in the conventional sense. That they weren't chosen for their weakness, as our killer might have perceived it. Whoever he may be, he isn't given to preying on the small and starving like a Zu Shenatir, or snatching painted boys from molly houses like a modern Jack the Ripper.

No. His is another, altogether different agenda. One which, even with Bunny's cache of borrowed documents before her, Sunny can't yet begin to fathom.

———

"I BELIEVE," Sunny says, dipping a hunk of flatbread into her tagine and washing it down with a mouthful of vin gris, "that I will pay a visit to the crime scene while I'm here. To the *dump site*, I should say. The flat in which the bodies were discovered."

"Oh?" Bunny loads a serving spoon with coriander rice and sprinkles it about her plate, betraying nothing.

"Surely you imagined I would do so, after reading those reports? Not one of those boys was from Birmingham, as I know you're aware. Someone *brought* them to that building. *Left* them there, to be found. How, then, are we not to ask: *why*? And more pertinently: wherefore *that* building? What does the space, the place, the city itself represent for our elusive mutilator? What, specifically, is its significance?"

"I was hoping you'd wonder about that," Bunny says, smiling now. There's a twinkle in her eye, Sunny sees. An impishness about the smile that feels decidedly un-Bunny-esque.

"Indeed. And on the subject of things about which I've been wondering..." Sunny raises her wine glass and sips like a hummingbird at the strange grey nectar within. Bunny, she's sure, will appreciate the pause for effect, the theatricality of the delivery. "What, pray, is *your* interest in this case? Don't tell me you thought only of *my* feelings, of *my* curiosity on learning of these killings. Not *even* you, Bunny, are as altruistic as that. You have a stake in this, somehow. In the *resolution* of this. The question is: *what*?"

A damask blush suffuses Bunny's apple cheeks – as ever it does, Sunny has discovered, when her efforts at subterfuge are brought to life.

She rallies quickly, however. "Alright. Yes. It's possible I might have... a bit of a vested interest in working out who did this one. Or in *you* working it out, I should say."

Sunny makes no effort to fill the silence that follows. When the crushing weight of social awkwardness becomes too great for her to bear, Bunny continues.

"The man who gave me the files. My police officer friend. I'm sure I mentioned he's been put in charge of the case?"

"You did," Sunny concedes.

"Did I also mention he's one of our players, up at Midgrove? A founding member, no less."

"You didn't, though it hardly comes as a revelation. You'll forgive me the assumption, Bunny, but I'd rather concluded that your rehearsal time with the early modern aficionados of the South Mercian suburbs comprised the lion's share of your social engagements, these last years."

"There's no shame in cultivating hobbies," Bunny says, low-key indignation emanating from her – the wounded umbrage of a family pet unjustly accused of defecating on the carpet. "But to return to my point, if you don't mind. The policeman, Duncan... he's one of our performers. He's been with us forever, he donates more than anyone to the capital fund for props and set design, and he's not afraid to let everyone know it... and he's just won the lead in next year's *Richard III. Richard III!*"

Sunny chews this over. "I'm afraid I fail to catch your meaning," she admits, when no obvious connection between this casting and the quintuplet of violent deaths presents itself.

"The man can't act!" Bunny's outburst is so sudden, so unexpectedly *loud* it causes the table to rattle and a tremor to spread across the surface of the stew. "He's playing Richard, and he's as convincing as a little eyas in a straw wig and an inflatable hump. He only got the part because he's a bully-ruffian who throws his weight around, and no-one wanted to antagonise him by telling him no or voting against him. Though I suppose that's *democracy* for you," she adds, bitterly.

"And?"

"And he shouldn't be our Richard! It's unfair, utterly unfair. He oughtn't be allowed to get away with it. He ought to be... well, taken down a peg or two. Taught a little humility. And I thought..."

Understanding dawns on Sunny, blinding as a nuclear sunrise. "You thought you'd call on me to solve the crime – the very *high-profile* crime – before he and the team he commands are able to? Then perhaps that you'd tip-off some of the more sensationalist of the tabloids as to the identity of the killer before placing the requisite anonymous call to the authorities, thereby ensuring the public humiliation – perhaps even the career downfall – of your counterfeit Richard? You thought, in short, that you might use me – *use me*, Bunny – to enact a petty vengeance upon a backstage rival, as if I were naught but an unwitting gull in some Midgrove rendition of *All About Eve?*"

"In my defence," Bunny says eventually, chastened but not bowed, "you do *enjoy* this detecting business."

"I do." Sunny swirls the remaining wine about the bottom of her glass, thoughtfully. "And lucky for you, I rather enjoy this new Machiavellian streak of yours. I daresay Richard himself would approve."

SEVEN

GRADY

It wasn't until he got home, sometime after 3am, that Grady realised he'd brought the old man's keyring back with him, the spiked plastic crown of that cheap souvenir rooster digging crescents into the skin of his thigh through the pocket of his trousers.

He'd have to get rid of it, and soon. The odds of anyone ever looking were small, infinitesimal, but it would be tempting fate to keep it in the house. And he'd have a hard time explaining away its presence if anyone ever did come knocking.

He climbed the stairs to the living room and, without thinking, threw the keys down onto the coffee table.

The Musician watched him. He was exactly where Grady had left him – staring back at Grady from the same spot on the sofa he'd been occupying earlier that evening.

Grady's breath caught in his throat. He'd forgotten the Musician would be there, still wide awake and waiting for Grady to come home. Forgotten that, in letting the musician move in, he'd made himself accountable to another person in a way he hadn't been since childhood.

It was a learning curve, a steep one. Especially now, with everything Grady had to do: every errand he had to run, every forgotten streak of blood he had to wash surreptitiously from his hands before he let the Musician see them. But he couldn't regret it. Couldn't begrudge it. It was nice, in a way, to be accountable to someone. To have someone stay up and wait for you to come home, no matter what you'd been doing outside of the house.

"Found this outside," he said, pre-empting the Musician's question – then picked up the keyring and shoved it back into his pocket. "Set of keys someone dropped on the pavement. I thought I'd walk up to police station tomorrow and hand them in."

The Musician smiled up at him, and Grady melted. Such a beautiful smile, the Musician had; that Grady should be the one to coax it out of him felt to Grady sometimes like a minor miracle.

Grady returned the smile.

"I missed you," the Musician said, without speaking. "Where were you tonight?"

Getting rid of the body of an old man we starved to death, Grady thought. *Trying not to worry about who Charlie and the others are going to send me after next.*

"Soho," he said. "It was only meant to be a couple of drinks, but then it turned into dinner, then more drinks at Annabel's, and... you know how it goes."

Still the Musician smiled, a world of love and adoration in his eyes.

"You're wonderful." The words were out before Grady could stop them.

The Musician's smile turned seductive, his curling mouth a sudden provocation.

Grady didn't resist – why should he? Only walked to

the sofa, bent down until his knees touched the floor and, taking the Musician's head between his hands, kissed him, long and deep.

The Musician's skin was cold and smooth to the touch, his perfect lips a frozen blue, and the flesh of his neck had begun to peel away, just a little, from the bone below.

But the kiss was perfect, nonetheless.

EIGHT

SUNNY

There is, to Sunny's very great dismay, neither a discernible police presence standing sentry at the entrance to the apartment building, nor a luminously fluttering ribbon of crime scene tape festooned about the outer brickwork.

Indeed, to the casual passer-by unfamiliar with the horrors so recently contained therein, Appletree House might appear entirely indistinguishable from the scores of other residential mid-rise block conversions in the vicinity: its glass balustrades no more cracked and blackened and its arches no more ominously Gothic than those of Goldsmiths Court across the road, or the whimsically-monikered Butterfly Point next door.

Sunny fancies, though, that she can still smell the blood that drenched the floorboards. Even through the luminol and fingerprint powder and industrial-strength cleaning products that followed in its wake.

A square, free-standing sign beside the entrance announces the building as the property of the developer Carson & Lambert – and its anticipated opening date as January/February of the year to come. Two- and three-bedroom units – the sign declaims that bit too eagerly – are still available for sale to interested parties, for a 10% deposit and a sufficiently robust credit history.

Whomsoever Carson & Lambert are, Sunny thinks, they may be forced to rethink their sales strategy in light of recent events and the attendant negative publicity. And perhaps to offer a discount on some of the more... sanguineous of their subdivided living quarters.

With no-one to stop her, she forces open the external door with a swipe of her palm and thereafter, encountering not so much as an elderly sentinel dozing behind a desk at the entrance of the spartan lobby, allows her nose to lead her along the hall to Flat 3. The scene of the crime.

That door, oddly, is not bolted tight, as she'd supposed the entryway to the site of so barbarous a multiple murder would be, so soon after the event. In fact it is unlocked, the thin pale-oak barrier opening inwards to reveal an empty room beyond, even as she presses down on the handle. An oversight on the part of the cleaning crew commissioned to sterilise and decontaminate the scene, perhaps? Or the work of a forgetful fledgling constable, summoned unexpectedly away from the job to a nearby tavern brawl?

The apartment within is... only an apartment: bare walls and barer floorboards, the residual blood and viscera odour she detected previously, stronger inside than out, overlaid with that same permeating chemical aroma left behind by the cleaners and the constabulary, but with no additional scent notes to complement its copper and coagulant hues. There is, that is to say, not so much as a trace of magick in the air: not a whiff, not a *molecule* of the salt and ozone flavour that heralds – and indicates after the fact – the presence of the supernatural.

She must deduce therefore that the remnants of the

slaughter so recently deposited here were the material consequence of an entirely *human* crime. No demon rent those men to pieces; no revenant risen from the grave thought to burn their skin with acid, nor lycanthrope commanded by the cycles of the moon. The perpetrator, whatever else they prove to be, is something equally as anthropoid, as *hominid* as the men whose lives they ended.

For a creature such as Sunny, so accustomed to the widespread public perception of the eldritch and the necromantic as more fundamentally barbarous than their human counterparts, despite so many millennia of cultural evidence to the contrary, the realisation is positively vindicating.

She bends to the floor, the better to examine what remains of the bloodstains embedded in the wood... and the accursed mobile telephone, which necessity has tethered to the brown leather holster at her hip like a Dodge City lawman's Peacemaker, begins to chime in shrill facsimile of The Devil Went Down To Georgia: Jonas' idea of a joke, and a further reiteration of his unwillingness to take her even remotely seriously, in spite of her great age and indisputable might.

"It's me," a low voice hisses in her ear through the device's symbiotic conglomeration of electricity and magnets, the complexity of which still leaves her dizzy. "Amir. Sean Keane's housemate?"

"I remember," she says, overcome with regret and self-recrimination at ever having thought to share with the boy her telephone number.

"Cool, okay. So, you know you were asking about his boyfriend? Mr Sugar Daddy?" The voice drops to a rustling whisper – as if Amir, wherever he is, has had cause to cover the receiver, the better to muffle his words. "You're not going to believe this, but he's *here*, in the house. He just, like, turned up outside five minutes ago, demanding to know where Sean had gone. And the *state* of him – you'd think he hadn't slept for a week from the bags under his eyes. I was worried he was going to hit me when I said I didn't know *where* Sean was and that I was just as messed up as anyone about him going missing. And then the guy starts *crying* on me! Full-on waterworks on the doorstep. I had to bring him inside and make him a cup of tea to calm him down. He's still in the living room now."

An interesting development in the Keane case, indeed. Might she trust Amir to interrogate this potential suspect in her absence? Might the Sugar Daddy be more biddable – not to say more talkative – right now, in his agitated state?

"And that's not even the weird thing," Amir continues, before she can ask. "The boyfriend... you're not going to believe who he is." He hesitates – to build suspense or to recover his breath, Sunny cannot say. "John Drayton! Sean's been going out with *John Drayton!*"

Silently, Sunny reviews the myriad Draytons with whom she's been acquainted: the jazz musicians and North American generals, the Jacobean poets and Olympian athletes. Proceeds to whittle down the list to only those Draytons now living, but finds no Johns remaining.

"The *actor*," Amir says, when she fails to deliver an appropriate response to the disclosure, and Sunny is sure she detects a hint of exasperation amid his whisper.

"I'm aware," she lies. And resolves to quiz Bunny later on the identity of this *acting* Drayton.

———

"OF *COURSE* I've heard of him," Bunny tells her, on Sunny's return to the manor house. "The man won an Oscar. Three Golden Globes. Two BAFTAs, an Olivier and an Emmy, and those are only the ones I can remember. There may be more besides. He'd be a shoo-in for an EGOT, if he could hold a tune."

Bunny opens her tablet – a device altogether more sophisticated than the grey, dust-coated desktop computer she'd once led Sunny to believe was her sole locus of interface with the digital world – and types, deftly, into its search engine. A gallery of images materialises upon the screen, each showcasing the same individual, whom Sunny infers must be the multiple-award-garnering John Drayton of legend: a square-jawed, bestubbled and conventionally handsome Black man of perhaps forty, smouldering for the camera across a succession of red carpets, foot-lit stages and smart-casual magazine photoshoots.

"Now *he* could carry off a Richard," Bunny says, enraptured.

"He may yet have carried off a *Sean*," Sunny replies. Then: "Do you happen to have his address?"

NINE

SUNNY

Bunny does not, after all, know where John Drayton-the-actor lives. It is however the work of but moments to persuade her to pry his address, through means of a judiciously placed telephone call and a light-touch application of the thrall, from the databases of the Midgrove Shakespeare Society's problematically talentless Richard: the senior policeman from whom the Appletree House crime scene photographs were acquired.

There are, of course, conditions attached to this act of apparent magnanimity. Sunny had expected nothing less.

"Wouldn't it be wonderful," Bunny says slyly, upon ending the call with her policeman, "if Mr Drayton were to pay a visit to our little group one evening before rehearsals? Perhaps give us a few pointers on inner monologue or character-building – something to help us along? And if he were to mention us to a few of his contacts in the industry afterwards, or to tag us in his socials... well, wouldn't *that* be a treat?"

"I'll see what I can do," Sunny tells her.

The primary British residence of John Drayton-the-actor is, happily for Sunny's purposes, in London: a mews house pied-a-terre in Southwark, a sliver of town she will forever associate with vengeful Norsemen, cruel but incompetent Anglo-Saxons and a bridge so structurally unsound that later Britons felt compelled to write a song commemorating its propensity to fall into the Thames. She elects to drive there – bidding Bunny adieu and re-entering the city just after nightfall.

Drayton's home is a rectangular block of whitewashed brick, midway along a narrow cobblestone street of dwellings likewise erected in Vitruvian salute to their Inigo Jones precursors. The tiny HAL-ish pupil of a video lens observes her from above the doorbell; undeterred, she presses the bell, and is rewarded only seconds later by the appearance before her of Drayton himself, as symmetrical and well-moisturised in the flesh as ever he was on camera, if redder of eye and more dishevelled about the shirt and trouser.

"May I help you?" he asks, his actor's voice mellifluous as an audiobook recording despite the malt and tobacco she detects on his breath.

"Sean Keane," she says. "I understand the two of you are... acquainted?"

She anticipates that Drayton will banish her from his doorstep. That she will have no choice but to thrall him, if she's to have any hope of engaging him in productive discourse.

She is mistaken.

"You know Sean?" he says, a quiet desperation overcoming his beautifully sculpted features. "You know where he *is*?"

"I'd hoped in fact that you might tell *me*. I've been looking for him," she adds.

He opens the door wider: a clear invitation.

"Come in, then," he tells her. "Please."

———

JOHN DRAYTON'S is not the first actor's drawing room to which Sunny has been privy through the ages. But it *is* among the tidiest: cleaner by some margin than the Pall Mall lodgings of Nell Gwynne, and less cluttered with Bacchanal and bootleg liquor than the Los Angeles mansions of Mabel Normand and Roscoe Arbuckle. Notwithstanding the half-supped bottle of Macallan left accusatorially open on the side-table, the greatest of Drayton's indulgences would appear to be books – the room, and indeed the entrance hall, a tessellating Modernist labyrinth of interconnected shelves and cases holding volumes from *Shuggie Bain* to *The Epic of Gilgamesh*. The latter of these gratifies her enormously – though she refrains from mentioning to Drayton, even in passing, her personal involvement in the events enumerated across its pages, during one brief but memorable sojourn in Uruk.

There are prints, Caillebotte and Edward Hopper reproductions framed and tastefully mounted on the otherwise naked walls; an acoustic guitar in maple and rosewood leaning insouciantly against a lower shelf.

"That's Sean's," Drayton says, on seeing her appraise the instrument. "A Gibson Montana, I believe. I found it for him in one of those dusty little muso shops on Denmark Street, but he likes to keep it here. He's never said as much, but I think he worries that if he takes it home, he might be tempted to sell it the next time he's... short of cash."

The ease and openness with which he references Sean Keane's presence in his life and home, the tenderness he makes no effort to conceal on speaking Keane's name... these strike Sunny as peculiar. Was Drayton not, after all, Keane's *secret* suitor? Was their relationship not, as Amir made so explicit, a clandestine – in the current parlance, a *closeted* – affair, conducted almost entirely out of sight?

"To clarify," she says, lest she commence her interrogation on false footings. "You and Mr Keane *are* lovers, are you not?"

Drayton's eyes widen. He struggles for a moment for breath and descends thereafter into a paroxysm of coughs and splutters shielded only partially by the application of cupped hand to parted lips.

"Sorry," he tells her, when finally he's able to speak again. "Nobody's ever asked me... quite like that before. I'm not sure anyone's asked *anyone* quite like that since the early '80." He glances briefly at the guitar; breathes deep of the faintly stale sitting room air, as if to steady himself. "But yes. Sean and I, we're together. He's my boyfriend."

"And yet, the two of you are..." She pauses, rummaging with magpie eagerness through the more contemporary extensions of her memory palace for the necessary lingo. *"On the down low?"*

Drayton's cough returns. Becomes a small but rumbling smoker's laugh. "Again: not the phrase I'd use. We're not out as a couple, and we might have been keeping things more cloak-and-dagger than we should have, but..." He stops himself. Drops his gaze again to the guitar. "No. You know what? No. That's not right, and it's not fair. *We* haven't done anything. *I've* been a fucking idiot, and Sean deserves better."

He snatches the bottle of Macallan from the side-table and swigs it neat, the gesture so reminiscent of a Bukowski barfly's guzzle, Sunny assumes it must be intended as homage. "There's no reason you should know this, but I came out when I was a teenager. Told the parents, the aunties... all the people who mattered, even the ones who didn't want to hear it. Went off to drama school with my rainbow flag and my Queer Nation badges, making sure everyone knew what a proud gay man I was. And then I graduated, and got an agent, and started going to auditions and trying to get cast in things... and I'm sure you can guess what happened from there."

"The agent recommended discretion?" she ventures. The Midgrove Shakespeare Society, surely, would never scatter any such obstacles along the amorous paths of *its* players: might Drayton have been better served by directing his talents toward the accepting embrace of a more provincial venue?

There follows another wistful glance to the guitar and a second affected swig of the whiskey, this one imbued with a certain Burton-in-*Virginia Woolf* flourish that speaks, Sunny suspects, of an ever-growing intoxication on Drayton's part. "Too fucking right she did. Cath's never made me get a beard, thank God, but she *strongly* indicated from the get-go that I'd do well to keep my private life private if I wanted anyone to hire me as a lead. It wasn't as bad when it was only TV work, but once you start doing films you have the studios sticking their noses in as well, trying to protect their investment. They wouldn't *let* me be out, if I wanted to keep working with them. They're racist bastards too, some of them. Persuading them to hire a Black guy feels Sisyphean sometimes. So, a Black *gay* guy? A Black gay guy with someone like *Sean* standing next to him on the red carpet?"

The beat of thick-soled footsteps on the cobbles outside strikes at Sunny's currently human eardrums like a flattened palm on a kettle drum. A visitor, approaching Drayton's door.

If he hears the steps, Drayton elects not to react to their presence. "But it's bullshit, isn't it?" he says, knocking back yet more of the whiskey, his voice growing maudlin, self-pitying. "None of it matters. *Sean's* what matters, and I should have told him so. Should have told *everybody* so, and so what if I'd had to go back to doing soaps and theatre? It's less money, but at least I could have taken him out for dinner or held his hand without looking over my shoulder. He deserved better, he *deserves* better than being someone's dirty little secret. If he'd *had* that, if he'd had someone less selfish and less of a shit to look after him, someone who treated him the way you ought to treat a partner... he might have stayed. Might not have felt like he had to run away from everything, and he'd be here with me now."

As Sunny might have predicted, the doorbell chimes: Drayton's clod-hopping visitor announcing themselves at last.

Inebriation slowing his reactions, Drayton pulls out his phone, swipes lazily at the screen and stares at the video image reconstituted thereon: a man of around Drayton's age, slim-hipped and pale-skinned in a well-tailored suit, a fedora of the kind Sunny might herself be persuaded to don obscuring the better part of his face.

"One moment," Drayton tells her, apparently satisfied with what the phone has revealed to him, and disappears from the sitting room to answer the door. When he returns, he brings the visitor with him: the man a little younger than she first imagined him absent his hat, thirty or thirty-five though prematurely balding, his straw-yellow hair thinned to a duckling's down at the crown and temples.

"Leo Grady," the visitor says, shaking Sunny's hand

more damply yet more vigorously than any right-thinking creature would deem necessary. "John's manager. I don't believe we've met?"

He tilts his soft-egg head in quizzical fashion as he squeezes, as if to take the measure of her – puzzled, it seems, to have discovered her there, under Drayton's roof.

She applies a painful pressure to his knuckles in return, her mind's eye glancing to the Bogart/Bacall oeuvre for this evening's nom de plume. "Vivian Rutledge."

"She's looking for Sean," Drayton adds, his expressive face registering no reaction to the hardboiled pseudonym.

Leo Grady's face, conversely, registers concern. "Johnny? Johnny, what have you been telling her?" He spies the now-verging-on-empty Macallan bottle. "Have you been drinking?"

Honestly, she thinks – *can you not* smell *it on him?*

Whereupon she realises: *she*, in fact, smells something, though on Grady rather than Drayton. Something dank and foetid below the citrus burst of soap and the cinnamon bite of cologne.

Old blood, and ordure, and decomposition. The cadaverine tang of human rot.

Drayton, lacking the acuity of her perceptions, seeks to reassure Grady. "It's *fine*, Leo. She knows."

"*What* does she know, Johnny?" Grady caresses the back of his own neck with one clammy hand, and she wonders how she could possibly have missed the stink of him when first he entered the room. It envelops him like miasma; illuminates his figure like a pestilent halo. "What have you told her?"

"About Sean." Drayton reaches for the bottle, raises it and swallows what dregs remain. For all the alcohol that must already be diffusing about his system, this last mouthful seems to embolden him. "About Sean and *me*. And I know what you're going to say, and God knows I know *you* think I should stay in the fucking closet until I retire, but I'm sick to death of hiding it, do you understand? I am *sick of it*. And when Sean comes back, *if* he comes back to me, I'm going to get down on my fucking knees and *beg* him to let me show him that I can be better for him. I'm finished hiding, Leo, do you hear me? I'm finished with it. So you can fuck off with whatever *advice* you're here to give me."

Grady's pink cheeks pale, then purple. "You're drunk," he says calmly, a thin patina of equanimity barely concealing his anger. "You're drunk and you're tired, and you've had a long week, which is why you're talking to me like this. That *must* be the reason, because I *know* you wouldn't be talking to me otherwise about pissing your entire career away so you can shack up with some Irish junkie you've known all of about three months. Even if..."

He stalls. Seems to apprehend, belatedly, that he and Drayton are not alone in the sitting room.

"Would you mind giving us a few minutes?" he asks Sunny. "There are some things John and I need to... iron out. Privately."

She looks to Drayton, anticipating objection. Drayton, though, is now slumped in the chair beside the side-table, his eyelids closed, the whiskey clasped between his thighs. He is, she senses, neither asleep nor unconscious – but appears nonetheless to have, as Jonas might put it, *checked out* of the conversation. She will get little else from him this evening, even with the thrall on her side.

Which is not say, however, that there no other investigative avenues to explore before the night is ended.

"Of course," she tells Grady.

Unobtrusive as a parlour ghost, she exits the sitting room and thereafter the house, crossing the cobbles to the paper-thin wisp of parking space in which the Morgan rests to deposit her phone in the glove compartment – and, in the relative seclusion of its passenger seat, to change.

Reconnaissance, she finds, demands of the reconnoiter a certain physical circumspection. An ability to fade unnoticed into the background of one's environment. Thus, as she so often does in such circumstances, she reshapes her outward form from hominid to feline: the long legs and opposable thumbs of the woman she'd appeared to be giving way to the keen ears and sinuous tail of a small black cat, so innocuous in this urban setting that not even the most paranoid of passers-by would look twice.

Nor *does* Grady look, when he spills from Drayton's front door onto the street and propels himself on foot from Southwark to the gentrified terraces of Denmark Hill. Not once – even as Sunny follows, unnoticed, at his heels.

TEN

GRADY

The altercation with John troubled him. But Grady knew better than to take the bloody diva at his word. Not even *John* would be that stupid, once he'd sobered up. The woman was more of a concern, though. Who *was* she, even? What was she doing in John's living room? And how in the hell had she known...?

It was almost a relief to hear from Piers after that. To have something else to worry about; something to focus on besides John's sudden urge to perform a public confessional, and what him doing so might mean for the both of them.

Piers was as rude and demanding as ever, naturally: not *inviting* Grady to the Belsham but *summoning* him, safe in the knowledge that Grady would comply whatever the hour.

Piggy-eyed, condescending bastard. Some of the left-leaning broadsheets already referred to his father, *Sir* Piers, as a gammon – it seemed to Grady only a matter of time before Piers Junior succumbed to the same fleshy-necked, vainglorious fate.

Grady would have something to say to the others about Piers, and the way Piers treated him, once the deal was sealed. Once Grady's own place in the pecking order was secured.

He set out for the Belsham almost as soon as Piers hung up on him, hopping on the Tube at Oval and alighting at Covent Garden station, the lifts disgorging him into a slow-moving swell of backpack-laden tourists congregating by the ticket barriers. He barged past them and on, up Long Acre and onto Langley Street to the Belsham's HQ. Then down: along the steps and through the basement entrance, where Eduardo the doorman stepped forward to buzz him though.

A dozen of the Prags were waiting for him in the Godwin Room, Piers included, though not Gaius: some lounging on the L-shaped sofa, others fiddling with chalk and cues around the snooker table, and one or two helping themselves to drinks behind the bar.

Piers reached him first, patting Grady on the back with a ham-fisted imitation of bonhomie that made Grady want to poke his piggy eyes out with a cocktail stick. "At last, the Pathfinder cometh!"

"Glad you could make it," said Charlie from the sofa. No bonhomie *there*, Grady noted. Feigned or otherwise.

"I came as quickly as I could," Grady told him, his tone less deferential than Charlie probably expected.

"We know you did, old man," Piers said, handing Grady a glass of something that looked like an Old Fashioned and smelled like cream liqueur. "*Thank you*, was what Charlie meant to say. Wasn't it, Chuck-Chuck?"

"Don't call me that." Charlie glared at Piers, and Grady wondered for a second if *he* might go for the Baby Gammon's eyes before Grady got a chance to. "Fuckwit."

He turned to Grady. "Anyway - now you *are* here, I've got some good news for you. *We've* got some good news for you."

"That right?" Grady didn't let himself hope. Not yet.

"Hell yes!" Piers clapped him on the back again, nearly spilling his own drink down Grady's sleeve in his excitement. "We've had a chat, me and Chuck-Chuck – and Gaius, obviously – and guess what? You're *in*, old man."

"Almost," Charlie said, raising a finger in the air to halt the Baby Gammon in his tracks. "You're *almost* in."

"That's what I meant." Piers looked wounded.

"What does *almost* mean?" Grady asked.

Charlie smiled, the curling of thin lip over whitened canines suggestive of something vulpine and hungry. "We *want* you, all of us do. We've voted on it. *Gaius* voted on it. It's just that some of us are a bit... uncomfortable about how little you've got at stake, versus the rest of us. You've not really got your hands dirty yet, have you? Haven't put yourself on the line, as it were. And if we're going to let you in – we need to know you have as much skin in the game as we do. That you're willing to do... let's say, *the wetwork*. Not just the clean-up."

Grady tried to tamper down his panic. To direct his spiralling thoughts and spiking pulse instead towards the offer, not the obstacles. Or rather, to the prize: the final outcome and the hundred vistas it would open up for him, not what he'd have to do to seize it.

"Who?" he said quietly.

"Up to you, old man," Piers told him, looking pointedly down at his drink and not at Grady. "Not sure you need any help from us on the *choosing* front."

Charlie rose from the sofa and clamped a hand of his

own on Grady's shoulder. "How about I tell you what we're after, for the next one? Then you can have a think and decide for yourself who might fit the bill."

ELEVEN

SUNNY

Not half an hour after returning to what Sunny assumes to be his home in Denmark Hill, Leo Grady leaves it again.

This time however Sunny does not track his journey to its conclusion – following him only as far as the Underground station into which he descends before turning around and retracing her steps, as quickly as her paws will carry her.

Wherever Grady is going, she reasons, he is likely to be gone – given his decision to travel by Tube – for longer than the few minutes it will take her to enter his trim little terrace and explore its darker crevices. And there *will be* darker crevices therein, of this she is certain. No man is without his feculent secrets who smells as Grady smells, whose clothes and body reek as his do of the spoiled flesh of others.

Grady's home security measures are robust. More so than one might expect of a property so modest by comparison with its four-storey Georgian neighbours. A surveillance camera, she observes from across the street, is trained upon the heavy, windowless front door. A white plastic box mounted on the brickwork advertises the intruder alarm system operating within. An electronic locking system bars manual entry to the property to all but those in possession of the password.

None of these, however, alone or combined, are sufficient to deter the truly determined home invader.

In demonstration of this point, she retreats to a nearby sweet briar shrub. Crouches, so as to evade the prying eyes of local residents... and changes, for the second time that evening.

And now she is arachnid: a wolf spider, round of body but lithe enough of multi-jointed limb to scuttle hastily across the road and slide unnoticed under Grady's door.

Such indignity, she considers ruefully as she squeezes herself between jamb and sill, would be wholly unbecoming of the god she was in ages past – when awe and veneration were all she knew and all she inspired in generation upon generation of her acolytes, from the ziggurats of Akkad and the Citadels of the Indus Valley to the barbarian kingdom of Alaric and the Tbilisi of Tamar the Great. Before the intercession of the fanatical preacher Ewart, who robbed her of so many of her once-significant powers and bound her permanently to this world. Who stole from Sunny, before his own annihilation, the first woman she'd ever come to care for as a friend.

At no point in that past did she conceive of a future in which she might slip willingly into the exoskeletal skin of a household pest in order to poke around the dwelling place of an offal-scented talent manager, for no more compelling a reason than that he may, perhaps, have murdered someone.

But here she is, regardless.

Once in, she reverts immediately to her most recent human form. Disables the alarm panel she'd been certain she'd find in the hall with a swipe of the hand and a smattering of syllables from the old tongue, and surveys her surrounds.

Grady's home is immaculate, aseptic – though the stink of him, the rot and putrefaction that clings to him intensifies, the deeper into his lair she treads. But for the odour, she might easily fool herself into believing she was inspecting a show home or, somewhat ironically given the man's profession, a sound stage assembled for a troupe of actors yet to utter their first lines. The living room's three piece suite is pristine, its walls embellished with such generic monochrome stills as might haunt the antechambers of a mid-range chain hotel, while the downstairs office bears no furnishing but a cantilevered chair and gunmetal desk, on which sits a closed and fastened laptop of a make not dissimilar to Sunny's own – the contents of which she vows to scrutinise more fully once the remainder of the house has divulged its mysteries.

The smell grows stronger still as she crosses to the kitchen: a gourmand's paradise of hanging knife sets, stainless steel fittings and copper bottom saucepans. It's strong enough, or so she suspects, to make a sensitive human retch; her more stoic olfaction, fortuitously, is no more repelled by the chemistry of death and its aerosol markers than by, say, the mildew musk of a fungal spore or the stagnant water of a vase of flowers left to wither beside a hospital bed.

She sniffs the air, tracking heat-spots of a fuller and more blossoming rot to the bowl of the sink and the marble of the worktop. Worst afflicted by some margin is the area immediately surrounding the refrigerator: a free-standing Italian model in a pastel blue of which Dan and Jonas, devotees both of Gio Ponti, would doubtless approve.

If the odour can be traced to any single source beyond Grady himself, then it is here.

She edges closer to the appliance. Seizes the gleaming chrome of its handle, and pulls.

Inside the refrigerator, neither wrapped nor crated but presented on a serving plate like John the Baptist's, is a human head. A human head whose sad brown eyes and thick dark lashes she has seen before, albeit only briefly, smiling out at her from the screen of Dan's tablet computer.

A head that was balanced until very recently on the shoulders of Sean Keane.

———

SHE HAS, of course, no mobile phone on her person with which to call for assistance. And yet, assistance must be sought, if she is to get to the bottom of this situation – if she's to uncover how exactly, and perhaps equally importantly *why* exactly, Sean Keane's decapitated head now peers out at her, lifeless, from the inner reaches of Leo Grady's refrigerator.

She needs Jonas, and she needs him soon. Before Grady re-enters the house and puts paid to the most pressing of her enquiries.

The absence of the phone and the communicatory immediacy it offers is a mild inconvenience. But Sunny has survived millennia without recourse to any such, or indeed any comparable device. She is not to be deterred.

There is, she estimates, but half a mile between her current location and the flat Jonas keeps in Brixton – where, unless she has much misjudged them and their nightclubbing proclivities, he and Dan are apt at present to be found. To bridge the distance herself, even in the rather too conspicuous forms of a cheetah or a bird of prey, would be to risk Grady returning in her absence, perhaps to remove or relocate the incriminatory head – and for the course of action she has in mind, the head must remain in situ, where she and more especially *Jonas* might access it at will. But there are other options, yet. More specifically: other *creatures* that might be persuaded to do her bidding.

A plan beginning to formulate, she makes her way out of the kitchen and back to the living room. Opens the curtain a crack and casts out her mind into the London night.

And there it is: the very creature she sought, its long snout buried in an overflowing bag of refuse discarded in the adjoining front garden.

A fox.

Not a sionnach, that particular genus of Celtic werefox with which circumstances, namely Ewart and his machinations, have forced her of late to renew her acquaintance. A red fox, Vulpes vulpes: as common in this urban wilderness as a squirrel or a hedgehog, or indeed a small black cat, and every bit as unprepossessing.

Silently, she beckons it to her. Bids it approach the front door and await her there.

Grady's home is not, it appears, replete with those scraps of paper and stray ballpoint pens which might facilitate the writing of notes. Sunny, however, has already observed the presence in the kitchen of a pile of receipts below the fruit bowl – and of a single black marker, attached by magnets to a wipe-clean whiteboard mounted beside the corpse-besmirched refrigerator. Thus equipped, she writes; her missive brief but unequivocal. Then opens the front door to deliver unto the fox its instructions; slides the note betwixt the animal's teeth, and dispatches it to Brixton.

She's heard it remarked more than once that a fox, if properly motivated, may run as fast as a greyhound or a racehorse over short distances. *This* fox, happily, bears out the maxim – the note it carries spurring Jonas to make the journey from his flat to Grady's door in only fifteen minutes.

"What am I doing here?" he asks as she ushers him inside – panting heavily and wiping sweat from his brow. He, like the canid, has been sprinting. "And how – and I cannot emphasise enough how much I want to know this – did you get *a fox* to shimmy up my drainpipe and come knocking on my bedroom window?"

"Foxes are excellent climbers," she tells him, showing him through to the kitchen. "Very sharp claws."

He ignores this. "Whatever this is, it better not take long. I didn't tell Dan where I was going. He's been brilliant with everything so far. All of... *this*." The boy gestures at Sunny, then at himself – the *this*, she infers, a typically elliptical reference not only to what Sunny *is*, but to the magicks Jonas now knows that he himself possesses. "Even so, though. *Just nipping out, there's a fox at the window asking for me* is a lot for anyone to take in."

"A few moments from now, I anticipate," she says, disinclined even to allude to the presence of the head until the boy has witnessed it for himself, "a dexterous Reynard will be among the least of your considerations."

He raises one sceptical eyebrow – but makes no attempt to press her further before she is ready to unveil what lurks, so to speak, behind the curtain. "If you say so. But so you know, we've probably got about half an hour before he realises something's up and starts ringing me. I left him arguing with a TERF on an MMORPG board, and you know how worked up he gets. It won't be long before one of the moderators boots him off the forum."

Little of this last statement would have made any sense at all to Sunny until recently. But since the deepening of her bond with the boy – and through him with the *other* boy, his erstwhile fiancé, and the technologies to which *he* is so attached – she knows better, and has learned more than ever she might have imagined of the digital world and its acronyms. Just as she has learned that there are those within and beyond that world for whom the very fact of Jonas represents a kind of provocation: an incitement to rage and violence untrammelled.

She is aware, of course, that the boy was once read by others as female, and was treated as such, in deference to the shape and arrangement of his primary and secondary sex organs at the hour of his birth. Is aware too that the public shedding of that externally imposed persona has been a source of contention for many in the boy's life – not least his father. For Sunny, a creature of no fixed corporeal abode, such preoccupations and the antagonisms they give rise to are, at best, bizarre. What business of hers, of *anyone's*, the pattern and nature of flesh and fat and hair distribution below another's clothes, no matter the social constructs that conglomerate around them?

The human genitalia, moreover, strike her as uniquely banal and uninspiring, irrespective of their specific configurations. Not least when compared with those of other species – the miraculously efficient avian cloaca, for example. Wherefore then the interest, the feverish *obsession*?

It makes, like so many things upon this earthly plane, no sense to her at all.

"Behold," she tells the boy, and flings open the refrigerator.

Jonas gasps. Takes a second to gather himself, and releases a low, long breath.

"Fuck," he says. "*Fuck.*" Then: "That's Sean."

"Yes."

"He's dead."

"It appears so, yes."

The boy pauses, lost for a moment in some mental calculation.

"And the person who owns this house," he says. "They did this to him? Killed him and put him here?"

"Perhaps. And perhaps not." She looks, very pointedly, to the contents of the refrigerator, and then to Jonas. "I wondered, in fact, if you might be inclined to help me find out."

The boy is no fool. He registers immediately her intent, the favour she intends to ask of him. "Oh, no. No, no, no. Not a *notion.*"

"I've yet even to pose the question."

"I already *know* the question. You want me to..." He lowers his voice to a hushed whisper, as if speaking the words represents a kind of blasphemy. "To talk to him – Sean. To bring him back and talk to him, so you can, like, interrogate him or something."

Never, in all her millennia, has she known a necromancer – nor any manner of mage – so thoroughly ill at ease with the scope and breadth of their power. The boy is positively bashful with regards the dispensation of his magicks.

"Surely you see the reason in it?" she says, ever resentful of his immunity to her more usual techniques of persuasion. "We are in need of answers vis-à-vis the circumstances of his demise, and right urgently. The lord of this rather petit-bourgeoisie manor in which we find ourselves will not keep away for long. And who better to confer that which we seek upon us than the victim himself, now we have at our disposal the... material by which to do so?"

This last clause contains a minor obfuscation. Only the lesser of necromancers – the least skilled, the least sortilegically endowed – strictly *require* the presence of a spirit's corpse to perform their conjurations, though proximity to the living body that was can certainly prove helpful to the process thereof.

And Jonas is, for all his reticence, no minor talent.

Quite how aware he is of his own capabilities, however, is another matter altogether. And for as long as *he* believes in the necessity of the bone and the flesh for the performance of the ritual, Sunny will gladly play along.

"It's fucking creepy," he says at last, though she senses underlying the protestation a certain willingness to be swayed. For such a boy as Jonas, *doing the right thing –* solving the crime and vanquishing the culprit – is a nigh-on irresistible compulsion.

And so it comes to pass that, with only the meanest of further bargaining on Sunny's part, the boy offers his begrudging assent, and utters unto the cold, meaty air of the open refrigerator those incantations devised, so very long ago, to restore the departed temporarily to the appearance of life.

With a rustle of silver and a crystalline sparkle, like water droplets hardening to ice, the intact ghost of Sean Keane appears, head and body, beside the refrigerator door.

And begins forthwith to scream.

TWELVE

GRADY

They wouldn't give him much to work with. But then, they never did. Just a set of keys, an unbranded sports bag loaded with the sort of personal protective equipment he associated with American crime scene investigators – the paper suit, the rubber gloves, the dual-filter respirator mask – and the address of a lock-up garage on a road he'd never heard of down in Colliers Wood.

The place Grady would take whoever he chose, once he'd chosen her.

They'd given him a car too, obviously: a Volkswagen estate in forgettable dark blue, second- or third hand and destined for the scrapyard as soon as Grady was finished with it. Piers had been the one to acquire it, paying cash to a guy in Stevenage whose name the Baby Gammon hadn't bothered to find out, and he seemed to Grady absurdly proud of his alpha-male resourcefulness in having done so. He'd also been the one to walk Grady down to the underground car park below the Belsham, to show him where the Volkswagen was stowed.

"Just this to go," he'd told Grady with another of those

grotesquely matey pats on the shoulder, his ham-hand clenched like the claw of a fairy-tale crone. "Then you're in, eh? Properly in."

"Can't wait," Grady had said, the sarcasm flying all the way over Piers' fat head.

Grady didn't know what the hell he was doing. Of course he didn't. But he settled on Leyton as a hunting ground: not the high street, with its uni students and respectable mosque-goers and middle-class gentrifiers, but the less obvious backways, where the homeless kids gathered in their sleeping bags amongst the heroin addicts wrapping belts around their forearms and the few working girls who still touted for business on the street, instead of on the internet.

He slowed the Volkswagen on the approach to the row of boarded-up buildings where they congregated, the condemned houses seeded in among abandoned store fronts and the greying memory of betting shops. Pulled the brim of his cap down over his face and drew up close to the pavement like a kerb-crawler.

An older woman came to him first: over forty but skinny as a teenager, the lines around her mouth grown deep and dry as arid riverbeds with tobacco and emaciation. *Too* old for him; too wary and too hardened. She'd lash out at him; she'd fight back. If he wasn't quick enough, she'd win.

Too risky.

He shook his head, waved her away, and the smile she'd plastered on for him evaporated, souring so quickly to a scowl that he worried she might swear at him, or spit.

Thankfully she did neither – just retreated to the doorway she'd been leaning against and waited for another, better prospect to appear.

A girl came to him next. This one *was* a teenager,

Grady thought: sixteen or seventeen under heavy makeup and curtains of greasy pink hair, her sickly white skin visible through the ladders in her tights.

He lowered the passenger window. Leaned towards her and, his vowels shortened and sharpened in a rough approximation of a Northern accent, asked how much she charged.

She told him, reeling off a menu of costs and options in the bored monotone of a chain-restaurant waitress, and he nodded *yes*. Leaned further across the passenger and opened the door.

Pathetically eager, she took her cue and slipped in beside him, filling the Volkswagen with a nausea-inducing coalescence of fried food, Poundland body spray and, under it, unwashed armpit. No pause for thought. No hesitation.

"Away we go, then," Grady said. And drove them on, to Colliers Wood.

THIRTEEN

SUNNY

"Would you mind reducing the volume a little?" Sunny asks the still-screaming ghost of Sean Keane.

The boy appears in death much as he did in life, albeit more translucent in hue; the tiled walls of Leo Grady's tasteful kitchen are blurry but visible through his iridescent skin. He is clothed, the memory of green woollen jersey and tight-fitting blue jeans snug against his spectral body, and his cheeks are smooth and shaven. His eyes, wide with terror, burn bright as a dying star.

"Give him a minute," Jonas chides her – still smarting, Sunny thinks, from the role she nudged him toward playing in Keane's temporary resurrection. "He needs to adjust."

For no more noble a reason than her own impotence in the face of it, she allows the screaming to continue, uninterrupted by further commentary. Several elongated, eardrum-rending moments later and the wailing abates – decreasing steadily in intensity and pitch before vanishing into silence, as if some public-spirited bystander has indeed turned down the dial on an unseen control panel.

"*Now* may I speak?" she says, when she judges sufficient time has elapsed – and when, more practically, Keane's white eyes have ceased their death-stare into the abyss and begun to focus instead on their immediate, animate audience.

"What's happening?" the ghost-Keane croaks through translucent lips. Then: "*Jonas?*"

"Yeah." Jonas is awkward, sheepish. His feet shuffle like the loafers of a father-to-be in a maternity hospital waiting room, circa 1955. "Sorry, man."

"I'm afraid," Sunny tells the revenant, conscious of the hour, "we find ourselves rather pressed for time, so any more complex questions you may have about your current condition will need to be addressed at a later juncture. Suffice it to say: yes, you are dead, still, despite this evening's brief reacquaintance with embodiment. And yes, you will be free once our business here is concluded to return whence you came. The precise nature of which, I might add, is no business of *ours*."

"What business?" The reply comes calmer and more measured than before. Whatever initial panic gripped Keane when first he manifested before them, it has already begun to ebb away. "What are you after?"

To Sunny's surprise, Jonas takes the lead in responding – perhaps, she thinks, to assuage his own guilt at having retraumatised Keane after the initial and surely greater trauma of his passing. Or perhaps simply because he doesn't trust her to handle the situation with the sensitivity he believes it merits. "We need to know who killed you. I'm sorry, I know this is shit – I can't even imagine what you must be going through, what you've *gone* through. But we just... we need to know. You know?"

To her yet greater surprise, Keane's mouth reshapes

itself into a melancholic smile. "You sound just like Dan. All that stumbling over yourself, trying to get a word out."

"Sorry," Jonas says.

Keane's gaze falls away from him and turns instead to the open refrigerator. To the decollated head – *his own* decollated head – therein. "It wasn't him. The guy this place belongs to, Leo: it wasn't him who did it, who did *me*. He's part of it, definitely part of it, and if there's ever a trial or whatever then he'd best be standing up there in the dock with the rest of them... but he didn't actually *do* it. That was... someone else."

"Who?" says Sunny.

The white eyes swivel back to her, striking in their intensity. He's no Godiva, this Keane boy – he lacks the Lady's cold fanaticism, the clean propulsive engine of her hatred. But he's angry all the same. Quietly furious below his sadness, now the initial fogs of fear and confusion have dispersed. "I don't know. The little shitehawk who did it, who stuck his fucking drip in me and stood watching me while I was dying like I was a fucking frog he was dissecting for Biology... I'd never seen him before that day. Not even sure I'd recognise him if I saw him now. I just know he wasn't Leo. *That* tool was long gone when your other man got me."

"Drip?" Jonas asks, beating Sunny to the punch. "Like an IV? Someone put an IV in you?"

The ghost-Keane grimaces. "Yeah. The sort you get in hospital, you know? Only... whatever was in it, it wasn't exactly medicinal. I can't say it improved my condition, having that flow through me."

"You may need to walk us back several paces, if we're to piece together what happened," Sunny says. "To begin, if we might, at the beginning. And proceed thereafter to Leo Grady and how you came to be... under his roof."

Keane regards her warily, mistrustfully. She's reminded suddenly, even in the absence of Bunny and her early modern enthusiasms, of the Swan of Avon, and of Eliot. *Those are pearls that were his eyes.* "Why? Why do you want to know?"

All revenants are different, as unique in death as the characters they were in life. But there are, nonetheless, certain calls to which all but the most placid of the after-living are drawn, like stray dogs to a whistle. Certain buzz-words to whose dark siren-song the dead delight in dancing. And Sunny has no ethical qualms about dispensing them, where necessary. "To avenge you, of course," she tells the boy, and who knows? It may even prove true, in the end. "Why else?"

———

IT STARTED WITH AN INVITATION. A job-offer, no less. One which Sean, who was as strapped for cash as ever, could ill afford to turn down.

Leo had accosted him one evening as he was leaving – no, as he was *sneaking out of* John's house in Southwark. Leo, whom Sean had known then only as John's manager: a little oily and unctuous, as he supposed agents and managers were professionally obliged to be, and more than a little prone to turning up unannounced at John's door when he and John were in bed or having dinner or just sitting on the sofa watching TV together... but mostly inoffensive. Benign, anyway.

"Hello," the guy had said, emerging from a pool of

shadow like a Victorian procurer in an *Oliver Twist* adaptation. "Have you got a minute?"

Sean, puzzled but certainly not at that stage afraid, had agreed that he had.

"Good." Leo had smiled at this: an oily smile, yes, but not a *threatening* one. "I've got... I guess you'd say a *proposition* for you. A gig, potentially. I know it's getting on a bit, but maybe I can buy you a coffee and we can talk it over?"

What kind of *gig* the guy could mean, Sean had no idea. He wasn't a performer, not an actor like John, and the possibility he might ever be *booked* for anything more creatively expressive than a week of office temping had never once crossed his mind. But he was skint, and he was curious, and a free coffee never hurt anyone, did it?

So, he'd followed Leo out of the mews onto Great Suffolk Street and into a late-night cafe on the ground floor of a nice hotel, and he'd ordered a mocha with four sugars and Chantilly cream on Leo's dime, and he'd let the man say his piece.

"I need a musician," Leo said, nibbling parsimoniously at the tiny biscotti that came with his espresso. "This club I belong to, they're putting on an event this Saturday: very small, very select crowd. I'm handling the entertainment, and I thought a bit of classical guitar might, you know... set the mood. John tells me you play. Quite beautifully, he says."

"I'm not a musician," Sean told him, wondering how Leo could have got the impression that he was. "I don't do gigs. I play for myself. No-one pays me for it. You want someone proper, someone who does that sort of thing. Events and stuff."

Leo had begun to fiddle with the frames of his expensive-looking glasses, his cheeks flushing an embarrassed pink. "Look. I'm going to be straight with you – we're both adults. It's not *just* a musician I'm after. I need someone who *looks* the part. A bit of eye-candy," he'd added, when Sean failed to immediately glean the subtext. "Not some hairy biker with a Stratocaster playing Wild Thing in the background – someone pretty. A cute little twink for the members to look at while they mingle, who also happens to be able to strum a few chords without going too off-key. I have a girl already: sweet thing from the Royal College, plays the cello. But I find myself short of a boy. And one can hardly take an ad out for *that* in The Stage."

Sean's initial reaction had been anger. Not so much at the proposition itself as the idea that a posh twat like Leo evidently thought of him as literal trade, a commodity to be bought and sold. "I'm not a fucking rent boy either," he'd growled.

Leo had physically recoiled, shrunk back in his seat. Afraid, maybe, that Sean was going to reach for him across the table or throw the scalding mocha in his face. When he'd finally got up the nerve to speak again, his tone had been decidedly more placatory, if not quite apologetic. "Jesus. Of *course* not – I mean, *obviously* you're not. And that's not what *I* want, anyway. I said *eye-candy*, didn't I? And that's all you'd be: there to be looked at while you played. Not *touched*, not... anything else. You'd stick on a tight t-shirt, bang out a few slow numbers, smile at the nice men who try to chat you up while you're working, then leave with your two grand in your pocket and nip back home to John. That's it."

"*How* much?" The prospect of a roomful of entitled queens and braying closet-cases eyeing him up and trying to grab his arse had been an ugly one, no question, and Sean had known he shouldn't countenance it. But two grand was a couple of months' rent, and Amir wouldn't – couldn't – afford to keep topping up the shortfall. And how bad could it *be*, if it was just one night?

"Two thousand. For the four hours – eight to midnight, though it's possible you'll be needed a little longer depending on how long it takes to wrap everything up. We're *supposed* to finish at eleven, but you know how these things go."

Four hours. Two grand, for four hours. How was Sean – how was anyone – meant to turn that down?

"And there's really nothing else expected?" he'd asked. Then, playing the best and only card he had up his sleeve: "Because if there is, and you've not been upfront with me... I'll tell John. And I can't see him being too happy with you about it, can you?"

Leo had winced, as if Sean really *had* reached out and slapped him. "There won't be any need for that, I promise you. Although, if we're on the subject of *telling people*... I *am* going to need you to sign an NDA if you take on the job. It's likely there'll be some rather... high-profile guests at the event, some recognisable names and faces, and I have to be certain for everyone's sake that nobody will go running to Popbitch or the tabloids about what they might or might not see on the night. I have to... make sure we're covered. *John*, I think, would understand that."

Yeah, Sean had thought, the one small advantage he believed he'd had in negotiating with Leo evaporating to mist. *He probably would.*

"What's in it, this NDA?" he said, trying to style it out.

"The usual. No saying what you see, that's the gist." Leo's hand had returned to his glasses, his fingers working the thin metal that ran the bridge of his nose. "And no telling anyone where you're going, *including* John. I'm especially serious about that part. It may sound extreme to you, even paranoid, but there are people's reputations potentially on the line here, their livelihoods, and it's my job to protect them. The same way I protect John. If you want the gig, if you *take* the gig, you're going to have to toe the line on that. Which means you don't talk about what you see or hear at the club, and you don't let on that you've been there, before *or* after. Alright?"

"I don't like it." Sean had willed himself to say no. To tell Leo to shove his two grand up his hole, get up from the table and storm out of the cafe. But he couldn't. Couldn't turn it down, couldn't walk away from it, not now it had been offered. "I'm not comfortable with it."

"And I really don't care about your comfort levels," Leo had countered, cold as ice. "All I need to know is, will you take the job, or not?"

———

SEAN HAD TAKEN THE JOB. And, true to his agreement with Leo and the ridiculous contract he'd signed, he hadn't told a soul. Not John, not Amir, not even Dan, to whom he'd taken to pouring out his heart in texts.

Leo's *club*, he'd discovered on the night, was a private members' place spread across three floors and the basement of a grubby white brick building in Covent Garden: somewhere Sean must have walked past a hundred times on his way in and out of Soho and Tottenham Court Road, but never noticed. Never looked twice at.

An actual doorman buzzed him inside and met him in the lobby, taking his jacket and guiding Sean and the battered Yamaha he'd had since sixth form along a warren of plush, dimly-lit corridors, through a set of heavy double doors – and into a small saloon-style area that reminded him, despite the comparatively opulent decor and the absence of cigarette mist and cheap cigar smoke, of the private room at the back of the Irish Club his dad would drag the pre-teen Sean to on a Sunday when he was growing up. Usually with more religious fervour than the old man ever directed towards Mass.

There was no-one in there waiting for him, to Sean's surprise. No sweet-natured cellist in a skimpy vest top getting ready to set her music stand up next to his; no tuxedo-wearing Bullingdon Boys with remnants of coke around their nostrils, who'd never in a million years believe that *Sean* had been to Oxford, too. No Leo either, come to that.

He turned around to ask the doorman... something: what to do, where to go, whereabouts to put himself until whoever was coming arrived and needed entertaining. But the doorman had gone. Slipped back out through the double doors, quiet as a mouse, leaving Sean alone in the bar.

Which was pretty fucking weird, wasn't it? Though probably not *so* unexpected, really. Posh twats like Leo and his mates never cared much about other people's time or convenience, or so Sean's experience of them at school and college had suggested. They showed up when *they* were ready, when *they* wanted something.

He considered ducking behind the bar and pouring himself a Cognac or a couple of shots of Belvedere. Then thought better of it and perched instead on the arm of the nearest sofa, the Yamaha resting at his feet and his gaze fixed on the doors.

"Not drinking?" said someone from behind him. Not a voice he'd heard before.

He whirled around, almost falling off the sofa in his

haste to see who was there, who was talking to him. There were three of them, gathered around the bar. A tall white guy with cauliflower ears and a shaved head who could've been a bouncer. A shorter and slighter blond guy in his thirties in a navy crew-neck sweater, a skier's tan and a Kenneth Williams sneer. And sandwiched between them, Leo. Chewing on his bottom lip and looking to Sean inexplicably nervous.

Where had they come from? He'd been watching the door more or less the whole time he'd been in the room – so how had they got in?

Was there another entrance, hidden away at the back? Or had they been there all along, and he, somehow, had missed them?

"Thought I'd wait until after the party," he said, trying not to let on that they'd startled him. "Didn't realise I was early."

The blond guy looked him up and down, as dispassionate as a butcher sizing up a cut of meat – which made sense, Sean figured, given why he'd been hired and what they were expecting him to do. There was something *off* about the look, though: something un-sexual, not at all to do with lust or desire or even with the blond guy deciding whether *other people* might consider Sean fuckable enough to make the grade. It didn't feel to Sean like being cruised, so much as like he was being measured for a suit.

Or a coffin, his brain had added, unprompted.

"Okay?" Leo asked the blond guy, sounding more diffident and more compliant than Sean had ever known him be with John, even in his oiliest moments.

The blond guy gave a nod – not to Leo, but to Cauliflower Ears. "Should be."

And before Sean could move a muscle or ask any of

them what they meant and what the hell was going on, the bouncer had a hand like an anchor on his shoulder and was plunging a syringe into the side of his neck.

———

"I WOKE UP IN A HOSPITAL BED," the ghost-boy says, his pearl-eyes smouldering. "Metal bars on both sides and a cannula on a drip-bag in my arm. No idea where it was, but it definitely *wasn't* in a hospital. More like the spare bedroom of someone's granny's house, you know? Flock wallpaper, and an old wardrobe shoved in the corner.

"Leo wasn't there then. But the other bloke was, the blond guy, and his henchman with the hypodermic. Standing over me, watching me. Like they were a couple of doctors, and I was their patient, and they were waiting for me to come round from an anaesthetic.

"I tried to talk to them, to shout at them until they told me what the fuck they were doing with me, but my throat wouldn't work, and I couldn't get my mouth open. And when they saw I was awake..."

The boy breaks off from his story. Stares into the refrigerator at his own, dead visage.

"What did they do?" Jonas asks, sounding to Sunny on the verge of tears.

Such a sensitive boy, still, she thinks, with a kind of wonder. *Even after all he's seen. After all he's* done.

"The blond guy didn't *say* anything," Sean continues. "Not out loud. But he must've done *something*, given a signal or something, because the other guy, the big guy... He walks over to the IV bag and starts messing with the button thing on the stand. The... what do you call it, the flow regulator? And I start to feel something in my arm from whatever's in the drip. A sort of burning, but freezing too, if that makes sense. Then it's not just in my arm, it's *everywhere*, like I've swallowed acid and I'm burning up from the inside. And *then*... I guess it was over, *I* was over. Whatever they'd been trying to do to me, they'd done it."

A leaden silence descends on the kitchen, punctuated only by the electric buzz of white goods and the metronomic in-and-out of Jonas' breath.

"How, then," says Sunny, choosing her words with care, "did you come to be *here*? Wherefore this icebox as your final place of rest?"

"I don't know." And now, unexpectedly, it is the ghost-boy and not the one still living who begins to cry; luminous runnels of phantasmal saltwater that fade to steam upon contact with the air. "I remember the bed and the room and the pain. I know what must've come after, that I must've... you know. Let go. Died. And I know I'm here now talking to you, and from the looks of me..." He glances down at himself, at the unavoidable translucence of his flesh and skin. "I've not got any *less* dead since it happened. But the in-between is murky, properly murky. Like a blackout. Like there's a hole in my mind where the middle bit should be."

Such amnesiac episodes, Sunny knows – such *murkiness* as the ghost-boy describes – are all too common a phenomenon among the recently-deceased. No doubt the missing connections will return to him in time, as the trauma of the initial passing evanesces: those days and hours separating the moment of death from the moment of reanimation.

For now, however, it may be that he has given them all he is able.

"I'd *like* to know, though," the ghost-boy adds, his eyes caught again by the blue-lipped head within the refrigerator. "Leo might not have done it directly, he might be able to kid himself that he's not a proper killer 'cause he let your man with the skinhead push the needle in, but he's still got blood on his hands, hasn't he? Blood on his hands and a dead fucking body in his kitchen."

"Maybe we should ask him, then." Jonas speaks quietly but firmly, his own fierce anger at the ghost-boy's fate simmering to what seems to Sunny an almost palpably scalding heat. "If the bloke who owns this place is the only one who can tell us what we want to know... maybe he's the one we need to talk to."

FOURTEEN

GRADY

He took the Volkswagen with him back to Denmark Hill once he'd finished with the girl, parking it a couple of streets away from the house and walking the rest of the way. He doubted anyone would look twice at something that nondescript left overnight on a road with so many people coming and going - it was Camberwell, not St Mary Mead, and hardly renowned for its overabundance of curtain-twitching spinsters. But a risk was a risk, and Grady owed it to everyone to play things safe. Owed it to himself.

The *best* risk-mitigation, he supposed, would be to get rid of the car altogether: to pass it along to a scrapyard or drive it out to the countryside, set it on fire and leave it to burn until any trace evidence inside had carbonised to undetectability. And maybe he would have done just that in other circumstances – but here and now, he was exhausted. John's outburst, the weird woman with her loaded questions, this last task Piers and Charlie had sprung on him... all of it had drained him. He wasn't sure he was capable of anything more demanding tonight than collapsing into bed with a glass of milk and a couple of diazepam.

And the Musician for company, if Grady could summon the energy.

At the doorstep, he deactivated the alarm on autopilot, his eyelids already drooping. It wasn't until he'd stepped inside and begun to disentangle his feet from his shoes in the hallway that he realised something – maybe more than *one* something – was wrong. That the lights in the kitchen, which he made a habit of switching off whenever he left the house, now seeped yellow and white through the crack in the closed door he was certain he'd left open. That the *living room* door, conversely, was now thrown wide where previously it had been closed; that the house itself, so rigorously perfumed with bleach and antibacterial agents since the Musician's arrival, now smelled faintly – very, very faintly – of fresh sweat and unfamiliar spices, of city air and muddied heels. Of other people. Other bodies.

There was someone in there. In the kitchen.

Myriad possibilities and attendant near futures played out before him. None of them good – the worst of them ending in violence, incapacitation, *discovery*. In Grady's own capture and eventual incarceration.

He had weapons, though. Not to hand, but he had them. And had them nearby, in the cupboard under the stairs. Long knives and blunter instruments: the tools of self-defence and more proactive measures besides, should the need for them arise.

Softly, stepping as lightly as his bare feet would travel along the floorboards, he approached the stairs, intending to reach out to the cupboard. Spread his fingers wide and willed his left hand forward towards the cupboard handle... and found he couldn't move it. Not a muscle.

He tried again: concentrated, imagining himself expanding and contracting what had only seconds before been perfectly functioning sinews... and, again, failed. Neither the hand nor the forearm to which it was attached would budge but remained instead resolutely static at his thigh and hip, as if held in place by some invisible lasso.

"I shouldn't fight it, if I were you," said a voice, drawling and female and entirely too close to Grady for comfort. "You'll do yourself an injury."

A creak of boot on board, a rustle of fabric unfurling – and a woman emerged into the hallway from the living room. *The* woman: Vivian whatever-her-name-was, the one who'd been with John that evening. Who'd *known* about John. Known about the Musician.

She wasn't alone, either. There was a man with her, a *younger* man, so young he might have been barely out of his teens: a pretty little twink like the Musician, but shorter and more wholesome looking, his baggy pants and long fringe suggestive of the thousand boyband hopefuls Grady had auditioned in the earliest days of his career. Glaring at Grady as if he hated him – yet waving his arms in the air like Simon Rattle. No: like a pillhead at a rave, circa 1999.

Big Fish, Little Fish, Cardboard Box.

"There is good news, and there is bad," the woman said, regarding Grady with a smile that sent a chill along his locked-up limbs. "The good news – and I think you'll agree it *is* good news – is that, for reasons I'd prefer we not go into, I'm quite unable to do you harm, much as I and my friend here might wish it otherwise. *He,* I should note, is entirely capable of reducing you to gelatine and mineral where you stand. Though I suspect he would prefer not to, on account of his conscience."

She looked briefly at the man beside her. Shook her head at him, a picture of sorrowful disappointment.

"The bad news, however – certainly for *you* – is that I

am fortunate enough to have at my disposal *other*... tools of the trade. Which is to say, Mr Grady, if you'll forgive the paraphrase: my friend and I, between us... we have ways of making you talk."

FIFTEEN

SUNNY

Tied to his own dining chair with the invisible binds Jonas has conjured and the rather more prosaic packaging tape the boy has uncovered in a kitchen drawer, Leo Grady is the perfect penitent: terrified out of his wits and beginning already to sing like a canary.

His loquacity is a consequence no doubt of the thrall Sunny has placed upon him, which compels him to confess his sins, and at length. His terror may be no more than a logical response to his current predicament: the bonds and the tape and the intruders in his home.

She would like to believe however that her present aspect has played some small role in augmenting, if not outright inducing his fear and trembling. For she has elected, for the purposes of this interrogation, to yet again transform. To appear before Grady as what Jonas is apt to describe as her *true self*: horns, hooves, blue tegument and all.

"May we proceed *without* the blithering and jabbering?" she instructs him, when his inchoate ramblings become too much to bear, and is pleased to observe how swiftly the thrall works its magic.

"Sorry," he tells her, swallowing down his blather. "I'll do better."

"I'm happy to hear it." She reviews the final sentences of his earlier and somewhat more coherent statements, with all their freighted allusions to *Piers* and *Charlie* and *the Belsham*, none of which mean anything to her or Jonas – nor indeed to the spectral Sean Keane, who glowers at their hostage from beside the refrigerator, imperceptible to Grady's human eyes.

"You were saying something about your club," Jonas snarls, sounding to Sunny dangerously close to abandoning his usual policy of non-violence in favour of rending Grady limb from limb and feasting on his flesh like a vexed Diony- sus. "And how your mates there are all pragmatists, which is why they've been going around killing people."

"Not pragmatists." Grady shakes his head, his tone condescending even in the grip of the thrall. "*The* Pragma- tists. Definite article, capital P. It's what they call them- selves, the guys at the Belsham."

"And the Belsham is the *club* to which you previously referred?" Sunny ventures.

"Yes," Grady says, his meekness returning – for *her* at least, if not for Jonas. "It's where they meet. Where *we* meet."

"What, so you can plan your next kill?" Jonas leans in until he and Grady are very nearly nose to nose and, with a calculation that takes Sunny quite by surprise, slowly squeezes together his fists.

Grady jerks in his seat, his arms tightening around his body as if in response to the fastening of a straitjacket. He cries out in pain, just once, and then is still.

His next breath, when it comes, is strained and shallow. "So *they* can," he says.

———

THE TALE he tells is convoluted and disjointed, Grady himself a far from reliable narrator. Nevertheless, Sunny is able to parse from his rambling apologia a roughly chronological sketch of what must have occurred, before and after Sean's demise.

There is she assumes – because there *always* is – not one beginning to his story, and thus to Sean's, but many: the diseased roots of a hundred pasts erupting through the soil of the present, and Grady their catalyst. The *specific* beginning however – that which *Grady* identifies as such – can be traced to an Alice Neel exhibition at a private gallery in Mayfair six months earlier, and an accidental meeting thereat between Grady and one Piers Delacourt, whom Grady had known at university, though never liked.

"He'd been dumped," Grady says, his nose wrinkling at the memory. "Piers... he wouldn't know a Neel from a blowup Koons dog. But he'd brought a girl there on a date, to impress her with his *impeccable* taste, and she'd ditched him – probably caught him sniggering at the breasts on some of the sketches. As soon as he saw me there on my own, he was all over me like a bloody wasp on a jam sandwich: asking how I'd been, what I'd been up to, whether I'd kept in touch with *the old gang*. Wheeling out every college reunion cliche under the sun. I kept trying to shake him off, but that's the thing about men like Piers, they won't *be* shaken. The idea that you might not want to talk to them, might not *want* to be in their company... it never occurs to them. Not for a second.

"He was already pissed when he came over to me, but it didn't stop him knocking back the Rieslings whenever a waitress passed him. When I finally managed to tell him I was leaving – when he let me get a word in edgewise – he was absolutely hammered, convinced we were the best of friends. And dead set on leaving with me, walking outside with me – just talking, talking, talking the whole way. Kept insisting we needed to have dinner, *really catch up*. In the end I let him take me to Saint Jacques for supper. I was worried he might follow me home if I refused."

Delacourt was a chatty drunk, not much given to discretion. Within moments of arriving at the restaurant, he'd dropped into conversation elliptical references to both *the club* and *the Belsham*: a name with which Grady had been unfamiliar, at least then.

"*He* brought it up." Grady's tone is petulant, the whine of a spoiled child caught with his hand in the cookie jar who insists nevertheless that another boy did it and not he. "I didn't ask him – I just wanted to eat and get the evening over with, so I'd never have to see him again. The *last* thing I wanted was to prolong the engagement, but he *kept* mentioning it: his *club*, his *place*. Mentioning it, then *apologising* for mentioning it and slapping a hand over his mouth, like he'd done something wrong or let slip some terrible secret when actually I couldn't have cared less *what* he did or *where* he went."

Even before the rock oysters and scallops had been served, however – though *after* he'd sunk several further glasses of Pinot Noir – Delacourt's remaining inhibitions had fled, and all discretion with them.

"I think I said something like, *so, what* is *this club, then?*" Grady says. "That was all he needed, that one tiny push, and then he was telling me *everything*: that he'd joined this incredible new club in Seven Dials, the Belsham. *Hugely* secret, *massively* exclusive, and he and some of the guys there were working together on some projects that were going to revolutionise basically every industry you could think of. To me, honestly, it came off like a TED Talk. The kind of thing you hear at tech conferences, normally about a year before the bubble bursts and everyone involved sees their shares bottom out. He started naming names, big names, and dropped in that Gaius – *the* Gaius – was a member, and all of a sudden my ears pricked up..."

No Gaius – *the* Gaius or otherwise – has succeeded in piquing *Sunny's* interest since the fall of Rome, and thus she is briefly at a loss.

Jonas, thankfully, is more au fait with the extant rich and famous. "Gaius *Hemingway*?" he demands of Grady, his eyes round as saucers at the very possibility.

Grady in turn regards Jonas' hands as one might a set of guided missiles. "That's right."

"You've heard of him, I take it?" Jonas asks Sunny. "Software billionaire dude, set up that clean water charity you keep getting leaflets pushed through your door about?"

"Naturally," she lies. "Who *hasn't*?"

"He invests in films. *That's* why I was interested." Grady raises his head, self-righteous even amid the thrall and the miasma of his own fear. "If Gaius hears about a project and it takes his fancy, he'll throw everything he's got at it. Blank cheque territory. It struck me that if I could engineer a meeting with him, chat to him about a few of the projects I've got lined up for some of our other clients at the agency... it might be very beneficial for everyone."

"You thought if you met him and sucked up to him, he'd give you money. Got it." Jonas' disgust is palpable. The boy may not be precisely familiar with Grady's line of work, but he knows a parasite when he sees one.

Grady ignores this, returning his attention to Sunny – though his gaze, she notes, never wanders *too* far from Jonas' hands. "That was why I went along the first time, after Piers invited me – when he told me who'd be there the next night, and that I ought to join him. It was Gaius. The *possibility* of Gaius."

Delacourt neglected to follow-up explicitly on the invitation he'd extended, to send a text or email confirming where and when they might meet the subsequent evening. But Grady – armed with the knowledge of the club's location, his own enthusiasm buoyed by the prospect of sharing a drink and a cigar with Gaius Hemingway himself – went along the next night regardless: Piers Delacourt's name and the details Delacourt had supplied when under the influence sufficient to persuade the tuxedoed Grendel on the door that Grady ought to be permitted within.

The reception he received once inside, however, was decidedly frosty.

Gaius Hemingway *was* there, or so Grady thought: draped in shadow in a corner of the club's lounge, his head turned away from Grady and the entrance. And others Grady recognised. Oliver Jarrett, CEO-in-waiting of the multinational Jarrett's Aggregates and Grady's contemporary at Cambridge, though they'd moved in very different circles. Ben Wollaton, founder of the XCLNT trading platform and grandson of 21st century robber-baron Sir Viv Wollaton, worth upward of £3bn at the time of the Rich List's last estimate. Charlie Newbury, next-in-line to inherit the IntraNational Rail Group and current editor-in-chief, if Grady recalled, of a libertarian literary magazine called Unbound, or Unfettered, or something along those lines.

All but Gaius stared at Grady like epicures startled by a cockroach in the lobster bisque, their expressions making plain just how unwelcome he was in this, the inner sanctum of their secret clubhouse.

And then there was Delacourt: shambling across the lounge towards him, his face a mask of mortification.

"He was embarrassed," Grady says. "Embarrassed he'd invited me, embarrassed I'd turned up. *I'd* embarrassed *him*, if you can believe it. And he was *desperate* for me to leave. Didn't actually ask me outright, but he might as well have done. Would have been less awkward if he had, instead of making me watch him dance around the houses, telling me he *didn't think I'd come* and that it was *really more of a members-only thing, you know?*

"And I would've left then. No doubt about it, Gaius or no Gaius. A man doesn't stick around where he isn't wanted. But then Charlie came over, obviously wanting to see what was what, and who this gatecrasher was that Piers had let creep in past the barricades. And it all took a bit of a turn."

Charlie – the Honourable Charles Newbury – was polite enough: enquiring who Grady was, what he did, how Grady had come to be at the Belsham that evening. And Delacourt had answered him, stumbling over himself in his efforts to explain away Grady's presence.

"I'm just leaving," Grady told Newbury, when the introductions and almost-pleasantries had run dry. "You needn't worry."

Whereupon, quite unexpectedly, Newbury had grasped Grady by the forearm, at exactly the moment he was turning to the door, and said: "Tell me, Leo: are you familiar with the Plank of Carneades?"

"The *what?*" Jonas asks.

And Sunny, at last – to her great jubilation – has something beyond her own dread visage to bring to the table. "It's a thought experiment. From one of the Hellenic Skeptics, if memory serves. Two shipwrecked sailors argue over a plank that will take only one of them to shore and the unluckier of the pair dies in the altercation that ensues, thereby raising the question, as so many ethicists seem wont to, of whether killing for survival might ever be a morally appropriate course of action. There are variations, too: more contemporary ones you may have heard of. *If a group of explorers stranded in the wilderness are forced to eat one of their party to survive, ought they to be punished for it? If a famine-stricken village kills and consumes its infants so that the adults of the village may endure, can we truly judge them for their crimes?*" She pauses. "You know... even as I say them aloud, it occurs to me that more of these speculations than one might expect concern themselves with cannibalism. Food for thought, indeed."

Jonas, however, his all-too-expressive face ever an open book, appears more confused than before. "I don't get it. A thought experiment?"

"It was a test," Grady says, sounding suddenly weary. "Charlie... he wasn't trying to talk philosophy or quiz me on my general knowledge. He wanted to know if I thought it was worth it – killing a man to save yourself. If *I'd* be willing to smother the baby for the good of the village."

SIXTEEN

GRADY

The sensations were quite unlike anything Grady had experienced before. Or rather, unlike anything he'd experienced *concurrently*: a strange, logically incomprehensible brew of narcotic, hallucinogenic and somnambulatory responses, each jostling for primacy along the speedways of his synapses. Were he equipped to identify and analyse each sensation individually in his current condition, he might have reached for some of the more obvious pharmaceutical and psychotropic comparisons: the racing-pulse adrenaline bolt of a dab of amphetamine; the sweat-inducing terror of a trip gone awry, bound limbs and chimerical visions of leering, blue-skinned monsters included; the irresistible, paradoxically mellowing drag of a mid-strength sedative.

Above all else: the ecstasy-like compulsion to talk and talk and talk, even to his own great disadvantage.

"Tell us about this *Charlie*," the monster had said, in the voice of a woman, while the man with the electric hands looked on.

What could Grady do but obey?

As he talked, he remembered: those early encounters in the club stitching together reel by reel in the private cinema of his mind.

Charlie asking him if he'd heard of Carneades and the Plank, as casually as he might have enquired about Grady's holiday plans for the summer – *then* asking him, when Grady replied in the affirmative, where Grady stood on the problem. What *Grady* would've done, in the sailor's place.

"Punched the other guy in the throat and then sailed off into the sunset, probably," Grady had told him, still salty from the snubbing he'd received. The humiliation of it.

And Charlie, unexpectedly, had laughed.

"You should stick around," he'd said. "Meet some of the others. Piers, old man: will you do the honours? Introduce our friend here to the gang?"

Piers' flabby mouth had fallen open so wide Grady had caught sight of his fillings. "Are you...? I mean, *of course*, yes. If you think it's a good move?"

"Wouldn't have said so if I didn't," Charlie had answered him, flashing Grady a smile that even at the time had seemed too broad and shark-like to be entirely trustworthy. "And why not come and find me afterwards, eh? Perhaps the three of *us* can have a drink."

Piers, apparently flabbergasted by the directive, was noticeably quiet during the hours that followed, making only the bare minimum of casual conversation. True to his word though, and to Charlie's instruction, he'd steered Grady around the lounge, making all the relevant introductions. Even Gaius Hemingway, absorbed in discussion with a man Grady thought might have been the Duke of Albemarle, had graced them with a nod and a cool, firm handshake.

Grady, though he'd tried with all his might to stop it

showing on his face, had been dazzled: struck almost as dumb as Piers by the sheer concentration of power, wealth and influence in the room. For a man forever and professionally on the peripheries of fame and fortune – almost, but never quite in reach of it, no matter how many parties and launches and screenings he attended, how many boardrooms he sat in and million-dollar contracts he signed at the behest of his clients – the proximity was intoxicating.

It may not have been where he belonged, exactly. But the Belsham, he was sure, was where he ought to be.

By the evening's close, when he and Piers had reunited with Charlie for the promised drink and Charlie had begun to hint in fits and starts at what the Belsham was and what it demanded of its members, Grady would have done almost anything if it meant he were allowed to stay.

<h1 style="text-align:center">SEVENTEEN</h1>

SUNNY

"The club isn't the *people*," Grady says – no longer obviously frightened, but descending gently instead into the kind of voluble stupefaction that is, in Sunny's experience, an altogether more common corollary of the thrall. "That's what you have to understand if you want to understand *them*. It's a philosophy, an idea – an animating principle. Hence the name, you see? *The Pragmatists*. They're all about realism, pragmatism. Radical consequentialism."

"And that's *what*, again?" Jonas curls his lip, the boy's pussycat effort at assaying a sneer. "For those of us who *didn't* do A Level philosophy."

"A rather tiresome ethical calculus much better applied in hindsight than in practice," Sunny tells him. "And neither so novel nor so interesting as Mr. Grady and his associates apparently believe."

Grady's answer comes flat and emotionless as a metronome. "Things don't have to be new to be effective. Sometimes the old ways are the best."

Sunny, whose own experience of *the old ways* has been characterised by a roughly equal ratio of premature death, skin-sloughing plague and street defecation to immutable wisdom and communion with the land, considers it politic in this instance to bite her tongue.

"What are they then, these *old ways?*" Jonas says. "What was it your mate Charlie sold you on, when he brought you into the fold?"

Grady smiles, a dreamlike glaze suffusing him. "A better world, and a place to belong. What does anyone want but that?"

———

CHARLIE, he tells them, led with the offer: a tacit invitation for Grady to join the club, even if he wasn't – on the face of it – *Belsham material.*

Grady, of course, had fallen over himself to accept.

Whereupon the provisos, what Grady had come to think of later as *the trials*, had risen to the fore.

Before he and the other members could *think* about admitting him, Charlie had said, Grady would need to prove himself committed to the club's larger aims; its practice and its manifesto. The other men, the founders like Charlie and the hand-picked additions who'd signed up thereafter, had proven already their dedication to the cause through what Grady came to think of later as *the holy trinity.* Namely: a shared belief and worldview; fidelity to those few core principles around which the club was built; and a significant and ongoing contribution of funds and means, in service to the enactment of these principles.

Though there was also, of course, the promise of mutually assured destruction, should any of the Belsham's work ever – by some terrible quirk of ill-fortune – go public.

Grady, alarmed by this suggestion of *destruction* but not

so alarmed as to be deterred from pursuing what Charlie had dangled before him, had questions. Chief among them: *what* aims and *what* manifesto?

And Charlie, with an astonishing candour and apparent lack of concern that Grady might, for example, go immediately to the police and report verbatim what he'd heard, had laid it out for him.

––––––––

"THERE ARE THINGS THAT NEED DOING," Grady says, the release of tension in his bound muscles and subsequent unwinding of his flesh putting Sunny in mind of a jellyfish at rest. "Things that propel us forward as a species, that improve the baseline state of being for everyone, everywhere. Breakthroughs in chemistry, biology, physics. Innovations in technology, materials science, engineering. Necessary adaptations in public policy and critical thinking. We all want them. We all *want* a better life, even if not everyone has the vision or the intellectual capacity to create it, to bring it to fruition. And those who *do* often find themselves... constrained by the limitations of the past."

Laws and legal precedent, for example, Sunny thinks. *Social norms. Historically agreed-upon behavioural frameworks.*

Those things which, by and large, prevent the madman running amok in the crowd with a knife and the would-be Frankenstein pouring electrical current into the reassembled corpse.

She understands immediately not only the point which Grady is trying, albeit somniferously, to make – but that which he *will* make in the moments to come. This is not her first monomaniacal rodeo, nor her hundredth – for what *visionary* tyrant, whether a Cromwell or a Periander or a Sargon of Akkad, *hasn't* sought to remodel the universe according to the revolutionary blueprint they devised? What strategist, what empire-builder, what grandstanding polymath *hasn't* believed so fervently in the necessity of the societal omelette that they've leapt headlong and enthusiastically into the breaking of the eggs?

Even the murderous preacher Ewart had wanted, in his way, to... how had Grady put it? *Build a better world.*

"I assume," she says aloud, her patience for Grady unravelling at the memory of Ewart, "that your happy band of Belshamites conceived of themselves as just such visionaries? And chafed therefore at those *constraints* imposed upon them by a blinkered judiciary? Constraints like – and I am, as my friend Jonas here might put it, just spit balling here – *try not to kill people in the name of progress?*"

At this *Grady* chafes, though the thrall retains its hold on him. "You don't have to like it to know that it's true."

"Sounds like a load of reheated Thatcherite wank to me." Jonas wriggles his fingers. For a fraction of a second, a pattern of unseen strings impresses itself into the fabric surrounding Grady's biceps, and the bound man winces anew. "Though I'd still like to know how any of this relates to Sean and what you did to him."

The ghost of Sean Keane, for so long merely a silent observer, nods vigorously in response. "You and me both, mate."

Sunny favours the dead boy with a thin smile that causes Grady to turn his head towards the refrigerator – or rather, from his perspective, the empty space *beside* the refrigerator. "Surely it's obvious? If we return to the

Carneades analogy: Sean was the sailor who drowned, so the other could live. Though I can't imagine the boy was the only sacrifice they passed over the fire to Moloch, nor even the first. Perhaps you can clarify that for us, Mr. Grady?"

EIGHTEEN

KATIE

There was nothing in the room: literally nothing. No windows, no furniture. Just four white soundproofed walls and Katie in the middle, trapped between them like a patient in a horror-film asylum.

When she'd first woken up and looked around her, she'd thought she was dead. That the psycho punter who'd picked her up in his car and then stuck her in the neck with a needle had finished her off, and she'd gone straight to hell. Or purgatory – a colourless nothing-place outside of time, built to hold people like her while they reflected on their sins.

Five minutes on, and her legs so weak she couldn't even push herself up from the floor, she still wasn't absolutely sure that wasn't true.

Hang on, though: *was* there something, up there in the ceiling? It could've been just a crack – a discoloured section of the whitewash that looked, from where Katie was lying, like a little black circle with a green dot in the middle. And it could've been nothing at all. She couldn't exactly trust her own senses right now, could she?

She thought maybe, *maybe* it was a camera. One of those spy cameras you could buy online and hide in a plant pot if you wanted to video someone without them knowing.

And if it *was* a camera: had the messed-up bastard who'd put her in here installed it?

Because if it was, and he *had*, it meant he was watching her right now, in this padded cell. And – she felt a wave of panic hit her like a closed fist to the stomach – it meant he was probably filming her, too. That he wanted a record of whatever he'd done to her *already*, before she came round a second ago. Or worse: a record of what he was *planning* to do to her later.

She had to get out. If this was a room, then there had to be a door somewhere, didn't there? One she could theoretically open, if she could work out where it was.

The whiteness of her surroundings making her vision swim, she tried again to get to her feet. Made it up onto her knees and then stumbled, falling flat on her face. She took a deep breath, getting ready to try again, and choked on it – the air she needed somehow... not in her lungs.

She'd never had asthma as a kid. But she thought maybe this was what it might've been like to have an asthma attack: trying to breathe, trying to get at the oxygen your brain and body demanded, but finding nothing in the tank. Feeling like your chest was collapsing, deflating on you as quickly as a party balloon; like however hard you tried to inflate it again the way you always had, every day, not thinking twice about it, the breath just wouldn't come.

What was happening to her? What had that mother-fucker in the baseball hat *done* to her while she'd been passed out in his passenger seat?

She craned her neck upwards, looking right at what might've been the camera: ready to scream at the maniac on the other end, to shout him out so loud he couldn't help but listen to her.

The words wouldn't come. There was no air at all there now.

And then there were spots behind her eyes, volcanic-black and silver, and she fell forward, and slept.

———

WHEN SHE WOKE UP AGAIN, the walls were gone. The *room* was gone, and it seemed to Katie that she wasn't *inside* anywhere anymore, but *outside*, in the open air.

Where the walls had been was landscape, closing in on her from all sides. Clear sky, unnaturally blue, hanging over a barren expanse of yellow sand. Leafless, bone-like trees – the kind that made Katie think of the Surrealist paintings her mum had loved and filled the house with back in Margate, all those Dalí deserts and Max Ernst Arizonas Katie had found so terrifying in the earliest years of her childhood.

An endless emptiness, all around her.

The sun pricked at her pores like porcupine quills. Below her, the sand was thick but gritty, painful and hot.

She smelled burning wood, and something dead and rotten passing over her on the breeze.

It turned her stomach. But there was an upside too, she realised – something positive to cling to even *here*, wherever this new *here* was.

Because she could breathe again.

She was sick and she was alone, and she'd been taken somewhere that definitely wasn't London and probably wasn't even England – that could've been fucking *Australia*

– by God knows who, who planned to do God knows what with her.

But she could breathe.

Once again, she tried to stand, and found that this time she could, if more unsteadily than she might have liked. Emboldened by this progress, she looked around her, scanning the (*desert? wasteland?*) for signs of life: a house, a vehicle, a Cattle Dog with an owner's collar... anything that meant she wasn't alone out here, in this patch of nothing.

And saw a shadow on the horizon: a high grey shape, unequivocally alive.

Moving, fast.

Coming towards her.

She blinked. Beads of sweat dripped from her forehead, forcing her to close her eyes. For a second – just a second.

Then the shape was closer, accelerating as it neared the place where she was standing, and she could see it for what it was.

She screamed. Couldn't help it.

The thing, the shape, was... the word her brain reached for was *scorpion*. A tall, long-legged scorpion, the blue-black-silver of an oil slick and at least as tall as Katie. Taller, probably – longer and more angular, its double-jointed limbs hyperextended to spindles.

Not *really* a scorpion, though. The body was too flat and rounded, the limbs too many. A crab, then? Or a *sort of* crab. A genetically engineered spider-crab, maybe. Something impossible, cooked up in a secret lab by a mad scientist.

It approached her, began to circle her, and she saw more details still: armoured plates and stilt-like legs, serrated claws like saw-teeth snapping at the air above. And eyes big as serving spoons, hovering on stalks above its shell.

Was it watching her? It seemed to Katie that it was. That it was preparing to strike.

She blinked again. Re-focused, willing herself not to let her fear paralyse her or turn her to stone.

It was maybe fifteen feet away now.

Then ten, and accelerating.

Then right there, looming over her.

She screamed again, right up into its insect face, but there was no reaction, no change in the movements of its body or the grotesque swaying of its stalk-eyes to suggest it had even heard her.

Instinctively, she raised an arm to fend it of, or try to. Then thought better of the idea, and turned to run.

Her feet were lead, her muscles frozen, but they took her weight. Propelled her forwards and away.

Not fast enough, though. Nothing like fast enough.

A chittering, a sound like displaced earth, and the shadow was on her again – *beyond* her, its proportions stretched and monstrous against the yellow sand.

She caught a flash of something hard and black and glistening at her shoulder. A stink like stomach acid and electrical burns at her neck.

She felt a tearing of skin; whipped her head around to see a pincer the size of a bear trap clamped around the meat of her arm, the blood it had released flowing down from her elbow to her wrist.

And, still screaming, she fell back into unconsciousness.

NINETEEN
SUNNY

It was clear early on in the relationship what he was to the Pragmatists, Grady tells them. They'd needed an errand boy, a lackey. Someone to do the dirty work they wouldn't muddy their hands with.

Piers wouldn't have come up with the plan himself, he reasoned; the lump head wasn't bright enough for that. When he'd gone off-script and invited Grady even temporarily into the fold, Charlie had spotted an opportunity to plug the gap in the Belsham's reach, and seized it.

And Grady, because even proximity to power like that was better than no power at all, had told Charlie he'd do whatever the club asked of him, if he was rewarded for it.

As Grady came to understand it, there were two current areas of research for the club. A brace of topics to which all members assigned much of their valuable time and many of their considerable resources: human longevity and health span, and sustainable physical security.

The first warranted research into the body, its limits and its capabilities – how far it could be pushed and augmented for what physical benefit, and how much it could take before it began to deteriorate.

The second meant understanding how properties and resources – and indeed bodies, of the appropriate kind – could best be preserved and protected from harm, should this ever prove necessary. In the event, for example, of a total or even partial social and environmental collapse likely to imperil populations and drive an angry minority to destruction.

Much of this research was in process already, conducted in collaboration with private labs, universities and think-tanks – though for the most part, the names of the club members involved were omitted from any formal press releases. There were other research projects, though, and other trials still to conduct: ones no ethics board would sanction, and not even the most morally flexible of governments would officially permit. Ones which, if made public, could theoretically bring the full force of the law, not to say some very heavy prison sentences down on any man who ever set foot inside the Belsham.

"They didn't actually see the police as a problem, obviously," Grady says, when Jonas queries why *these* possible consequences didn't concern him, or Charlie, any of the club. "We're talking about some of the richest men in the country, the sons of princes and sitting MPs. They don't just think they're untouchable – they *are* untouchable. Nobody who wanted to keep their job would try to arrest them, let alone prosecute them. You know that thing Trump said about shooting someone on Fifth Avenue and getting away with it? It could just as easily apply to them. So no, I wasn't worried. Not about that."

Grady's inaugural mission, as the Belsham's foot soldier

and apprentice, came soon after that first conversation with Charlie in the shadows of the club lounge – mediated and commissioned by Charlie himself, as all subsequent missions would be. Grady wasn't told then, nor at any point in the future, which of the Pragmatists had the greater hand in which project; when speaking for one, Charlie spoke for all, though Grady drew his own inferences around which members would be liable to benefit most and most immediately from which project, which strand of research.

That first time, the task was straightforward, though very far from easy: Grady was to find an old man whom no-one would miss, and deliver him to the clubhouse. And when, eventually – a day, a week or a year thereafter – the Belshamites were finished with him, Grady was to find a way to dispose of the body, inconspicuously.

———

"I WENT TO A FOOD BANK," Grady tells them, oblivious to Jonas' revulsion and to Sunny's frustration at his snail's paced delivery. "It seemed the most obvious port of call. A lot of old people use them, don't they? And it's often the ones with no family, nobody to look after them at home."

He'd found his subject – the *right kind* of old man, hungry and desperate – on his second visit: Grady's hood pulled up and baseball cap down, so as to show as little of his face as possible to anyone who might otherwise have cause to remember him later. The guy was sallow, tall and wiry, with a boxer's knuckles and a surprisingly full head of grey hair; in his early seventies, Grady estimated. Like so many of the older people at the food bank, he seemed embarrassed to be there. Ashamed – and who wouldn't be? – at finding himself in need of a handout. Fortunately, unlike a lot of the others, he was reasonably sociable, his lively banter with the greasily ponytailed man charged with handing out food parcels over the counter giving Grady all the information he required to be sure the old guy fit the bill.

Lived alone: check. No family to speak of: check. Didn't get out much: check.

Got a little bit lonely sometimes in his flat with nobody to talk to: check, check, check.

"I followed him home," Grady says, and Sunny is briefly concerned, though not *terribly* concerned, that Jonas might actually lose what tenuous grip remains on his temper and break the cutthroat's arm, through mystical means or otherwise. "All the way to Wembley. It was one of those terrible Brutalist tower blocks, despair oozing out of the concrete. I went inside right after him, waited five minutes, then knocked on his door and got him with the hypodermic before he could ask me what I wanted."

Grady's actions immediately afterwards were more ad-hoc – more spontaneous and infinitely more humiliating than they should've been, and much more so than they *were* at his subsequent abduction and disposal scenes. He'd phoned Delacourt, that witless gull; begged him to drive out to the tower block in the shabbiest car he could access and bring with him the biggest trunk or suitcase in his wardrobe, ideally one on wheels.

To Grady's great relief, Delacourt had done just that, though not without a moderate amount of grousing. And the pair of them had packed the heavily sedated old man away into Delacourt's enormous hard-shell Montblanc, wheeled him out of the building to Delacourt's car and, following a brief encrypted text exchange with Charlie, driven him to the site of a run-down former brewery just off Brick Lane – where, Grady would learn later, the more clinical of the Pragmatists' research projects were conducted.

"I don't know the ins-and-outs of what they did to him," Grady says. "Just that it was to do with cell senescence and caloric deprivation. There was a strong interest within the club in how effectively a more radical approach to fasting could encourage cellular rejuvenation, particularly in older subjects. How it could slow down the ageing process, where calorie deficits are low enough – reverse it, even. The science is solid, I'm told. But obviously there are limits to what one can do, if one abides by current protocol."

Sunny watches a dozen expressions of puzzlement and revulsion slide and settle across Jonas' face as he puts together the pieces of this last disclosure. "You starved him to death. For *science*. You took an old man out of his home, and you starved him to death so your mates could see how long it took him to die, on the off chance that starving *him* might show *you* lot how to keep from getting arthritis."

Grady has no response to this, no comeback or rejoinder. But still, he continues his tale.

Eventually, he recounts, he reclaimed the old man's corpse, disposing of it according to the club's instructions. Before that, however, Charlie had issued him a *further* set of instructions: to retrieve for them not one, but five new living bodies. *Young* men this time, young and fit and strong. Men who seemed like they might have been in the army, or at the very least a CrossFit gym; who looked like they could withstand a little punishment.

"Charlie said... He *said* they wanted to road-test a new

security system," Grady tells Sunny, instinctively knowing better even in the clutch of the thrall than to look *Jonas* in the eye. "He and the guys were starting to think about prepping – doomsday scenarios, you know? Underground bunkers for the end of days, that sort of thing. And especially what to do about what Charlie called *swarmers*: people who might be outside the bunkers, trying to get in. One of the guys was looking to develop some new weapons systems to use as deterrents. Chemical dispersal mechanisms, new bullet and blade types, detection and tracking radars, LDEWs – that's lasers, the sort that slice through metal. Things to keep the swarmers away. Or deal with them if they managed to break through."

In the further reaches of Sunny's mind, a small and far-off bell begins to chime, insistently.

Five men. Blades and burning chemicals and other dicing implements besides. Lasers that could surely slice through flesh as easily as butter.

Five men, mostly homeless, snatched from all the corners of the country. Five bodies ripped apart, abandoned in an unfurnished apartment in a Midlands city.

Surely it cannot be coincidence.

"You went outside of London to find *these* men, I presume?" she asks their captive.

If Grady is surprised by this guess, no evidence of it is apparent on his tranquilised face. "Yes. To Brighton and... other places. We didn't want to shit where we ate."

"And when your friends had finished testing their devices on these human guinea pigs – you again disposed of the bodies? Perhaps in Birmingham, far from view of the capital?"

Though Grady remains unfazed, Jonas' mouth gapes wide at the specificity of the guess.

"What the fuck?" This from the ghost of Sean Keane, equally agog.

Sunny dismisses them both, directing every modicum of her attention towards Grady.

"That's right," Grady says, slow and mellow. "Ollie Lambert's dad owns a couple of properties up there – it was his idea to use one of the empty flats. Ollie's. They've not been getting on lately, and he's developed a bit of a grudge against the old man. I think he thought it'd be funny, dumping a load of bodies there. And that it'd hit Carson & Lambert in the wallet – that there'd be so much bad publicity, his dad and Brian Carson would have to pull out of the development and lose whatever they'd invested."

And so another circle closes, Sunny thinks. *I really* must *tell Bunny.*

"A prank." Jonas is positively snarling. Were he sionnach like their former comrade Tara, he would have torn Grady's head from the man's neck with his teeth long before now. "You dumped five dead bodies in a flat *so your mate could get back at his dad?*"

"And engineered their demise, lest we forget," Sunny says. Then, catching the ghost-boy staring meaningfully at her from his resting place, adds: "We have, I realise, failed to address the *true* elephant in the room. Might we deduce that the late Sean Keane served a similar purpose, for the rest for your utilitarian friends? That he was, perhaps, an unwilling test subject, for some ethically dubious pharmaceutical or other?"

Grady's mouth droops. "An immunosuppressive. Gaius' people are developing it – trying to. The trials they've done on mice with it showed a massive increase in lifespan, something like 50%. But they haven't been able to..."

"Test it on people," Keane's ghost finishes for him. "I wonder why."

"Sean... reacted badly," Grady continues, obvious. "And quickly. Too quickly."

"Which doesn't explain why you've got his head sitting in your fridge," Jonas says.

"I have a theory." *All* heads, spectral and corporeal, turn to Sunny.

And indeed, she *does* have a theory, albeit one drawn not from millennia of observation of the human condition but from a recent rereading of Agatha Christie's *Nemesis*. Grady, she has come to realise during his confinement, has something of the Clotilde Bradbury-Scott about him whensoever Keane is mentioned. It's there in the quiver of his lip; the forlorn creasing of his forehead. An unconscious signifier of an emotion so deeply ingrained it resists even the pressure of the thrall.

"Yes?" Jonas prompts her. "And were you going to tell us what it is?"

She exhales, loud and disgruntled; disheartened as ever by the boy's impatience with the pregnant pause. Then to Grady, in the finest Jane Marple she can muster, says: "You loved him, Mr. Grady – isn't that so? And yours was a jealous, covetous love, never more so than when you were forced to watch him on the arm of your biggest client, day in and day out. But it *was* love, nonetheless. You saw Sean Keane and you wanted him for yourself. But he only ever wanted John, didn't he? Only John – never *you*. I expect he barely acknowledged *you* were there, whenever you paid John one of your unexpected late-night visits.

"I won't pretend to understand precisely what possessed you to suggest him as a subject, when your friends put in their request. Anger, perhaps, at his refusal to see your worth, to share in your feelings? Or was the desire to possess him, even in death, simply too overwhelming? Perhaps killing him, even indirectly, was the nearest you believed you'd ever come to making him yours.

"Regardless: that's why you kept him here afterwards, is it not? Why you took his murdered body and claimed it for your own. Why he's here, in the room with us now."

TWENTY

SUNNY

"Jesus Christ." The ghost of Sean Keane appears, improbably, to pale and sicken. "That's... He was keeping me here for *that?*"

Jonas offers the ghost-boy a small, sympathetic grimace. "Sorry, man. Not really something anyone wants to hear, I guess."

Grady's dulled gaze flits from Jonas to the refrigerator. "Who's he talking to?" he asks Sunny, the thrall thickening his tongue.

"Never you mind," she tells him, and he quietens, his expression impotently mutinous. "All that's required of *you* at present is affirmation of the hypothesis we discussed. I'm right, am I not? That *is* why you delivered the boy unto his executioners, and why you've preserved his remains here, in your home – when, I expect, your friends at the Belsham anticipated your disposing of them elsewhere?"

Grady reddens, in his yoke. "Yes."

She turns to Jonas. "And thus, we have our answer. *Answers*, in fact, and many more than I might have foreseen. Our work is done."

"I'm sorry, what was that?" The ghost-boy's demeanour morphs from horrified revulsion to pure outrage. "Your work is *done*, you say? Because it very much looks to *me* like your work has only just fucking *started*. That gobshite *killed* me. *And* all those others he was on about. He needs locking up, putting away. You can put him in the *ground*, as far as I'm concerned."

"He's not wrong," Jonas agrees.

"Who's not?" says Grady.

Sunny rounds on Jonas and Sean: the boy living, and the boy dead. "Were neither of you listening a moment ago? Even in the event of our summoning the local sheriff and his watchmen to investigate the contents of Mr Grady's refrigerator, we'd be hard pressed to persuade them to charge him, given his connections and the involvement of his... confederacy. And on the very slim chance he *were* to be loaded into a Black Maria and driven to the cells, he'd be released the moment he placed a call to his solicitor. With an apology from the Commissioner, I'd wager, if not the Home Secretary herself. "

"We don't know he was telling the truth about his mates – about them being untouchable," the ghost-boy says, sullenly. "For all we know, he could've made the whole thing up to cover his own arse. All that stuff he was saying about his *club* and the money and the power and whatever... it could be a load of Keyser Soze shite to throw us off the trail. Distract us from the fact that he's a murdering, necrophiliac cunt."

"Would you care to enlighten him," Sunny asks Jonas, "or shall I?"

"Enlighten *who* about *what?*" says Grady, watching the unfolding of the exchange with the glassy-eyed bafflement of a drunken spectator at a tennis match.

"She's right," Jonas tells the ghost of Keane. "Sorry, I know it's shit and not what anyone wants to hear, but... he can't actually lie. Like, *physically* can't. The thing she's done to him, the hypnotising thing – it means he *has* to tell us the truth, or at least what he *thinks* is the truth. So, unless he's genuinely delusional, which seems a bit unlikely given he definitely *did* take you to that club and there definitely *were* other blokes there... I think we have to believe what he's saying. About the police, as well as the rest of it."

The ghost-boy hesitates before responding – though not, Sunny observes, for *terribly* long. "Kill him, then. Keep doing that... whatever you're doing with your hands, but harder. Squeeze the life out of the fucker."

"We don't believe in killing," Jonas says. Then, with a glance at Sunny, adds: "Well... *I* don't, anyway."

"He's a fucking murderer!" Keane's ghost is quite insistent on the matter. "I don't care if he actually pulled the trigger himself or not. He's killed seven people!"

"The revenant *does* have a point," says Sunny, who in truth would have very few qualms about Jonas ending the monster Grady where he sits, were the boy so inclined. "Mr. Grady has indeed done away with seven people. It seems rather lenient simply to let that slide, whatever one's position on the nuances of natural justice."

"Eight." All eyes turn to Grady, who meets at least four of them drowsily. "You forgot the girl. I mean, she's probably not dead *yet*, technically. But still."

The thrall is strong in this one, Sunny thinks, her private language tainted anew by the Hollywood blockbusters through which she has suffered.

"The girl?" Jonas twitches, his demeanour that of a subterranean rodent just alerted to a bright light up ahead in the tunnel. "*What* girl?"

TWENTY-ONE

SUNNY

The peregrine falcon is among the fastest creatures in the animal kingdom, capable of speeds of over 240 miles per hour. It is in this form that Sunny traverses the light-polluted skies separating Denmark Hill and Colliers Wood.

"You're quicker than I'd be, even if I took the car," Jonas had insisted, practically throwing her onto the pavement beyond Leo Grady's front door. "And I need to stay here with *him*," he'd gestured at this to the captive Grady, still firmly secured to his own kitchen furniture. "I don't trust that duct tape to hold him on its own."

"And if I'm set upon by goons in the carrying out of this civic duty?" she'd argued. "Were this *my* clandestine inquiry into the frailties of the human condition, I like to believe I'd invest in at least a minor contubernium of armed enforcers. And our Gaius Hemingway, it seems, has no shortage of such funds as might be required to fund a private legion."

The boy had actually *smiled* at this suggestion. "You'll cope, I'm sure."

"Despite my *very well-documented* inability to defend myself in violent struggle? I am literally prevented from vanquishing my antagonists, should they come at me – the laws of my... place of origin decree it so. Ours is not a human judiciary, and I can tell you now, such arbiters as we have do *not* take kindly to transgression. I shall have no self-defence clause to fall back on – if I am attacked, I can only stand and endure. I'm positively helpless."

To her great irritation, the boy's smile had only broadened. "I believe in you. And I've seen you in action – you're about as helpless as a tank, even if you can't actually kill anyone with your bare hands. And you're immune to stuff like poisons, aren't you? Whereas I'm *not*. So, either you go and be a hero, or odds are you'll have two incapacitated bodies to deal with – mine *and* this girl's. Plus a multiple murderer to go chasing after, once Jeffrey Dahmer here wriggles out of his chair."

And thus, with poor grace and no small amount of bitterness, she had taken to the heavens.

———

"THE GIRL, THEY'RE TESTING HER," *Grady had told them, the confession tumbling out of him. "Testing her body. What it does to her."*

"What what *does to her?" Sunny asked him. "With what will they be testing her?"*

"Mycelium. Fungus. Or... fungal roots, I think. Gaius' people, one of his R&D teams – they found this new kind of fungal root out in Australia. In the middle of the country, you know? The remote bit, where there's nothing but rocks and heat. Nobody had seen anything like it before when they first came across it, that was what Charlie said. I don't know why they were looking for it, if they even were looking for it or if they stumbled onto it by accident... but it blew them

away when they tested it. When they saw what it was, what it could do. It's potent, you see. Unbelievably potent."

Jonas mulled this over. "Potent how? What does it do?"

To Sunny, the answer was obvious. *"It's a weapon, yes? Another weapon, like the bullets and the lasers and so on. Yet more ammunition for the coming siege your friends antici-pate. I would imagine this Hemingway hopes to turn his magic mushroom into some airborne armament or other – a poison gas or an asphyxiant, something of that ilk."*

Grady nodded. "Yes."

"Which makes the girl...?" Jonas said.

"Another guinea pig," Sunny told him. "They're poisoning her. Gaius Hemingway *is poisoning her, so that he might watch her as she dies and make a note of it upon his clipboard."*

———

FOLLOWING the directions Grady has given her, albeit under duress, she proceeds to her target: an automobile repair garage on an unusually quiet light-industrial street in the southernmost reaches of the city. The building is sand-wiched between a grocery wholesaler and a small ware-house, barred and bolted, that purports to accommodate frozen shellfish, kelp and phytoplankton – though Sunny detects on the breeze no evidence of marine life therein, chilled or otherwise.

The garage itself is a squat triangular edifice clad in bone white aluminium, its shape reminiscent of the prefab-ricated Christian churches she's spied of late in the more evangelical regions of the United States. It is also shut: the red steel door marked as its Entrance firmly locked and very visibly chained, and the rectangular sign that dangles from it confirming the premises as *Closed for Essential Maintenance.*

Neither sign nor locks and chains, of course, present for Sunny any greater obstacle than the security measures in place chez Grady. Though in truth, her earlier protestations weren't *entirely* for show: she is, despite her well-honed stealth and enviable turn of speed, somewhat nervous at the prospect of facing whatever hostilities lie within the garage. Her knack for survival throughout these last, fraught millennia has depended in no small measure on the eschewing of direct conflict except where absolutely unavoidable; of staying, if not entirely *out* of the line of fire, then at least two or three rows back *from* it, where other bodies might soften the hail of bullets. Callous, even bellicose she may have been – as Bunny seems never to tire of reminding her – and keen she may once have been to incite *others* to acts of violence on her behalf, but stupid Sunny is not. Wherever the fates have conspired to force her into battle – with the preacher Ewart, say – she has been sure to enter the fray shoulder-to-shoulder with her own army of capable combatants. With those who *could* fight; who *could* kill.

(Even if, she thinks before she can prevent herself from doing so, these brothers- and sisters-in-arms could themselves also *be* killed: pounded to cooling meat by a fist with the force of a freight train, or cut to bloody ribbons by a reaching claw. Like the foxes and their human confederate, back in Gallow.

Like Miranda, strong and pitiless though ever she was, at the end).

Nevertheless, Sunny darts forward. Dives, and comes to land beside the sealed garage entrance.

And here, yes, there *is* an odour: moist and earthy,

undeniably fungal. Further confirmation, she must presume, of the veracity of Grady's tale.

The street is empty – and thus she changes where she lands, her wings shrinking to spider legs and her beak to chelicerae until, arachnid once again, she is able to slip herself unseen below and through the steel front door, just as she slipped through Grady's.

Behind the door, to her initial confoundment, the garage is... only a garage: an airy, open-plan room designed around an automotive repair proposition. There are tyres, propped up against family-sized yellow oil cans and unplugged power cables; a row of wrenches, coil spring compressors and grease guns, suspended from a tool wall that appears, from her arthropod vantage point, the length and width of *Guernica*; two hydraulic lifts, presently free of cars but evidently intended to accommodate them. There is even, she observes, a waiting area for customers: a half dozen plastic chairs, an unoccupied reception counter, and a fish tank into which a client might gaze while they await the rejuvenation and return of a cherished vehicle.

A second and closer inspection, however, reveals the a lie: that this is not a working garage, but a *simulation* of such, and nothing more. It is a stagehand's rendering, mimicking the appearance of a lock-up at a surface level, but neglecting to attend to more minor multi-sensorial details. The smell of the oil implied by the presence of the canisters, for example. The hung-up overalls and stained chamois leather that a working mechanic might leave behind at the end of the workday. The living, swimming fish one might expect to populate the tank.

Everything is that bit too *clean*. That bit too perfect to be convincingly real.

Again, she changes – reshaping herself human, or into

the approximation thereof that she's so favoured lately. And at this greater bipedal height, she spies it: another door in the interior wall, its frames and paintwork blended in such a way as to obscure from the observer its defining edges, its beginnings and its ends.

It is, she thinks, a hidden door. A *secret* door, no less.

She approaches, slow and quiet. There is, of course, no handle to be found upon the aperture, no jutting interruption of its trompe-l'œiel effect – and no obvious means therefore of accessing whatever space might lie within.

She leans her weight upon it, the better to gauge its structure and its density. To take the measure of its cordons, so that she might decide upon a strategy to breach them.

And the door, under this most meagre of pressures, swings open – onto a short, narrow, claustrophobically low-ceilinged corridor of pure white brick and resin floor. A German Expressionist's corridor, torn from the reels of a horror picture; a picture set, perhaps, in a 19th century hospital or an abandoned asylum.

Yet another door marks the corridor's terminus: a heavy looking, windowless Angstloch of a hatch affixed to the floor, its shape and position connotative of a Dumas oubliette or a Pontefract dungeon. *Here* there are handles – wrought iron and surprisingly ornate given their surrounds, their appearance bordering on the baroque.

This threshold will not, she senses, be so easily breached. The application of brute force will likely be required.

Conscious of the surveillance devices she can neither see nor hear, but which must surely be monitoring every inch of the passage, she moves swiftly to the hatch. If any such devices are indeed watching the area, she reasons, they must perforce be watching *her* now – and hence, any armed guards Gaius Hemingway has engaged to carry out his bidding will soon be coming for her, their pistols raised. Speed must be her watchword.

Quicker than the eye, though with no small amount of elbow-grease, she wrenches the hatch free of its mooring and, in the absence of any stairs or stepladder which might ease her passage, drops down ten feet into the space below, landing cat-like on the balls of her feet.

Another room confronts her. This one is undeniably a prison cell, as starkly white and windowless as the corridor above, and containing nothing at all but a girl: *the* girl, whom Grady snatched from the streets of East London. She is terribly young, and scantily clad, and apparently unconscious, her small form curled in upon itself in the centre of the bare tiled floor. A corona of blood radiates out around one thin shoulder; the flesh from which it flows is torn. Bitten, to Sunny's very great puzzlement, as if by some large and savage animal.

Why the girl is cataleptic would be immediately apparent to Sunny, even had she *not* been appraised already of Hemingway's nefarious intentions. For the scent of the man's engineered cocktail of poisons is as pervasive down here, in its way, as the olfactory afterimage of decay that lingered in the makeshift mausoleum of Grady's kitchen.

Cataleptic fortunately is *all* the child is, despite the obvious blood loss and the chemical toxicity that envelops her. Her chest still rises, if more erratically than might be expected of one who was simply asleep; beneath their fragile lids, made electric blue with cosmetics and the spectre of veins, the muscles of her eyes flicker left and right in tandem with the firing of neurons and the energetic rattling of her limbic system.

At least for now, she lives.

Sunny springs forth, traversing the cell in a single bound, and bends to Hemingway's prisoner, her human body primed to lift the girl up and onto and around her shoulders.

Whereupon she senses movement – not from the girl, but from above. Footsteps: the clamour of boot on resin and, after a moment's pause and a satin cut of flesh through air, on tile.

She raises her suddenly altogether *too*-human head, preparing to meet the cusp of a baton or the barrel of a Glock. The glare of a hired mercenary intent on her subduing.

And sees instead the smiling, faintly waxen face of a trim and neatly coiffed white man scarcely older than Jonas – his hooded sweatshirt and tapered cargo trousers indistinguishable from the many that hang in Jonas' wardrobe.

It's not a face she recognises. But there is something faintly familiar about its contours nonetheless – about the composition of the smile, the stretch of skin about the mouth. Perhaps, she rationalises, because she has seen it before; has dimly registered its presence, but failed to take note of the man to whom it belonged. On screens and tablets; on broadsheet pages, and the covers of a hundred magazines.

"Gaius Hemingway, I presume?" she asks, though the question is rhetorical, for who else *could* this be, standing before her in this torturer's chamber hollowed out of the earth?

The half-familiar face splits into a boyish grin that tickles unpleasantly at the roots of her memory. "Look at you," he says, his voice a rich bass-baritone that fits not one iota with his smooth cheeks and adolescent's garb. "You haven't changed a bit."

And it's then – at precisely the moment that his flesh begins to ripple, his hands and feet to harden into hooves and the bony points of his barb-like horns to rise up from the surface of his newly blue-green skin – that Sunny realises who he is, this creature masquerading as a man. And why he looks now – in this, his *natural* state – so very much like her.

"Nor have you," she tells him, letting her own extremities thicken, her own horns pierce the no longer *quite* so human flesh under which they've been concealed. "And it's been, what – five hundred years? I'd call that something of a coup for both of us."

TWENTY-TWO

"No. No, I'm not doing that to him. Please, just... stop, alright? Just stop."

The sweet-faced man with the floppy fringe was talking to himself. And if Grady still wasn't entirely lucid, still wasn't completely clear-headed even with the fog that had descended over him beginning to lift – the fog the blue-skinned monster had *draped* over him like some torpefying shroud – he was at least sufficiently alert to be perturbed by this development.

"Who is it you think you're speaking to?" he asked, not expecting a response. If the guy was so far gone that he was arguing like that with himself – or with the Abominable Snowman, or the ghost of Anne Boleyn, or whoever it was he thought was arguing back – then the odds of him stopping to listen to *Grady* were slim. The kid had made it pretty obvious before the full-on psychosis had kicked in just how much contempt he had for his hostage.

His head whipped around to look at Grady – still trussed up like a bloody turkey in his chair. It struck Grady that he was startled. Like he'd forgotten Grady was still there with him in the kitchen. "No-one. Nothing."

"I can *hear* you," Grady persisted.

"Yeah? Well, *I* don't want to hear *you*. So I suggest you shut your mouth, unless you want that tape to gag you as well."

His pretty eyes blazed, giving every indication that he'd be happy to not just silence Grady with the duct tape but smother him to death, if getting away with it were a possibility.

That was that, then: if Grady was going to break out of his restraints, out of the kitchen and away from this maniac, it wasn't going to be a question of talking the maniac around. Active listening, empathy, building rapport... none of the usual hostage-negotiation strategies were going to get the job done here. Not when the guy hated him this much.

If Grady was getting out, he was doing it bodily.

The guy turned away, apparently so disgusted with his hostage he couldn't bear to look at him for longer than a few seconds.

Now, Grady thought. *Now* might be the time to start trying his luck.

He wriggled his wrists against his ties, testing the pressure against his arms and chest, and found it... less than it had been. The tape was still binding him, sure. But the *other* force, those invisible ropes the guy had used to bind him – was it his imagination, or were they looser?

Was the pretty boy starting to lose whatever sorcerer's grip he had on Grady, now he was losing his mind?

The tape itself wasn't tight – wasn't even that adhesive, after so many years of disuse in the back of the drawer. Clearly tying Grady up *that* way had been a bit of an afterthought. Could it be that the man – and the monster –

were more used to relying on their other methods to keep people where they wanted them?

But then: maybe *those* methods were reliant on the kid being able to concentrate on holding his prisoners in place. And presupposed he wouldn't get distracted by any imaginary friends.

Slowly, quietly, Grady twisted one arm against the tape. It slackened, then gave – creating space enough for him to unshackle first the corresponding biceps, then the elbow, and finally the hand.

A hand that, if it moved fast enough, could pry the remaining loops of tape from his other arm, and then from his legs, and – assuming the young guy didn't hit upon a reason to turn around again – release Grady entirely from the chair.

And there didn't seem much danger of that last thing. Because the young guy definitely *was* distracted.

"She'll be back soon," he was saying, addressing the empty air in a secretive mutter that was nevertheless ear-splittingly audible to Grady. "And believe me, she'll know what to do with him – with all of them. She might not always make *great* decisions, and I'm not saying I agree with where her head's at sometimes, but if there's one thing she's good at, it's vengeance. There'll be a way to stop them, take them down. There *will* be. And I promise you, she'll figure out what it is. Okay?"

That's me he's talking about, Grady thought, willing the tape not to rip too loudly as he pulled it free of his trouser leg. *Me and Charlie and Gaius and Piers. All of them. All of us.*

He wants us dead. Or she does, that fucking demon with the goat-feet and the devil horns. The kid just doesn't want to do it himself.

I really need to get out of here.

Carefully – so carefully – he rose from the chair, letting the tape fall away. He made no sound, or so he thought, no creaking of wood or tell-tale scraping of metal on tile – but there must have been *something*, some change in the atmosphere to alert him, because suddenly the pretty boy was whipping back around like someone had shouted his name, and he was *staring* right at Grady, his mouth wide open in shock.

There was no time to hesitate or weigh up the options: the kid's hands were weapons, Grady had seen enough to be sure of that, and the moment he shook off the surprise that had him frozen to the spot and *pointed* them at Grady, the moment he squeezed his fists together the way he had before, it was over. *Everything* was over.

So, Grady did the only thing he could think to do, right there and then. He dove for the top drawer of the cabinet less than two feet to his left, the *open* drawer he used to store some of the sharper of his kitchen implements; grabbed the longest and most pointed of the Sabatiers he'd ordered especially from Thiers... and thrust it hard into the pretty boy's soft throat.

It didn't connect.

Instead, to Grady's surprise, it stalled mid-flight – grazing the skin, but halting a fraction of an inch before it penetrated the flesh below.

He'd stopped it. The kid had stopped it.

Not completely, though. Not enough to turn the blade on Grady or send it ricocheting up into the ceiling. Whatever *X-Files* superpower the guy had been channelling when he'd pinned Grady to that chair, it wasn't working at full capacity.

Not with his arms by his sides and his fingers still.

"Move your hands," Grady said, his eyes flitting from the pretty boy's fingers to his panic-stricken features and back again, "and I'll cut out your throat. One tiny step forward, that's all it'll take. There won't be time to stop it happening."

The kid blinked: once, twice. Cocked his head very slightly to one side, like he was listening out for something Grady wasn't privy to, and then licked his lips and swallowed, the motion closing that bit further the already infinitesimal gap between the knife and his throat.

"No," he told Grady, staring him down, the tip of the blade at his skin rendering him hoarse, "you won't. You haven't got it in you."

To this, Grady had no immediate reply. And, through the silence he might have filled with a pithy comeback or a forward-flick of the knife, the boy ploughed on.

"You don't know what it's like to actually kill someone. Probably you *think* you do, because of everything you helped your mates do to other people at that club, but you don't. You might've found those people and knocked them out, you might have played delivery boy... but you weren't the one who stuck the needle in Sean's arm, were you? No matter *what* fucked-up things you did to his body afterwards when he couldn't fight back. And you weren't the one who chopped those other guys to pieces, either. You've never been a proper killer, I don't care what you've been telling yourself. You've never been the butcher. Just the bloke who drove the cattle to the slaughterhouse."

"You don't know what I can do," Grady said, finding his voice, a part of him wondering why he was talking at all. Why he felt the need to justify himself, when he could've been slashing the pretty boy's throat and making a run for it. "You don't know me."

"I don't need to." The pretty boy held Grady's gaze, inexplicably unafraid despite the knife and the blood. "I've known enough people *like* you to smell it on you, the cowardice. People who go along with things because some dickhead demagogue told them to, and who think that if they throw enough bricks through the right windows then they'll earn themselves a place at the table. They make me sick. *You* make me sick. But you don't scare me. Not these days."

"Your mistake," Grady said, pressing the knife upwards into the pretty boy's skin. Pushing back harder against whatever weakened force-field the kid was still commanding to hold it at bay.

Now the pretty boy gasped. *Now* his eyes widened, as the small nick below his chin deepened to a laceration.

Then shifted focus, suddenly – as if he'd just caught sight of something immediately over Grady's shoulder.

"Sean doesn't think so," he told Grady, the words tumbling out in a low whisper. "Though maybe you should ask him yourself. He's standing right behind you."

It wasn't true. It *couldn't* be true: Grady knew that, logically. But nevertheless, against all his better judgements – and no more able, suddenly, to control his racing thoughts or the movements of his limbs than he had been earlier – he followed the line of the pretty boy's gaze, craning his neck and twisting his upper body so he too could see what the pretty boy was seeing: a small, bright kernel of something in the burned-out hollow of his heart hoping he really *would* see the Musician there, whole and breathing and waiting for him.

Which he wasn't, of course. There was nothing there but yet another patch of empty air.

Then the blade of the knife, no longer in Grady's hand but turned towards him, its bloodied tip hovering barely a millimetre from his chest. And the pretty boy, one hand clutching at his wounded throat and the other clenched into a fist, the wrist below it moving minutely up and down and side to side in time with the motion of the blade.

The kid had tricked him.

Which meant it really *was* over. There'd be no getting away now: nowhere for Grady to hide until the monster came back from wherever she'd been and decided what to do with her prisoner. How to *take him down*.

Him, and all the others at the club.

And if by some miracle she let Grady live, set him free, even – well, what then? Not even a thing like *her* could handle all the Prags, with all the resources *they* had at their disposal. Piers and the weaker ones, maybe; the ones with less money in the bank and fewer contacts to call on when a thornier problem arose. Probably she could take *them* down if she put her mind to it. Not everyone at the Belsham was like Gaius, after all; not all of them could command a private army.

But some would emerge unscathed from whatever she threw at them. And the ones that did, once they worked out who'd ratted them out... *they'd* come for Grady, too. There'd be nowhere for him to hide *then*, either.

Nowhere safe. Nowhere.

Perhaps the pretty boy was right, Grady thought. Perhaps he *was* a coward, after all.

And, remembering the feel of the Musician's cold skin under his fingertips, he stepped forward, into the knife.

TWENTY-THREE

SUNNY

In fact, it's been nearer *six* centuries since Sunny last crossed paths with the creature who now calls himself Gaius Hemingway, in the shadows of a Florentine piazza. He'd gone by Niccolò then – though she suspects many more pseudonyms, and indeed faces, have come and gone for him between that day and his adoption of the Hemingway persona.

She hadn't cared much for him then, nor in the millennia that preceded the encounter. And nothing about the circumstances of their current reacquaintance suggests she will have cause to re-evaluate that opinion.

"You're the mastermind behind this bargain-basement Ishii Unit?" she asks him in the old tongue, surreptitiously positioning herself between his newly towering proportions and the rather smaller and more fragile form of the bleeding, unconscious girl on the floor. "My understanding was that *Gaius Hemingway* was a kind of Bill Gates figure. A computer programmer made... well, perhaps not made *good,* given some of his more recent enterprises, but certainly made *wealthy.* An entrepreneur. And moreover, though I

concede this was perhaps more of an inference on my part –
human."

It's curious, she thinks, that she can neither smell nor
sense him, as she can those others of her kind who've abandoned their homeland in favour of this particular plane of
existence. So often they shine out at her like points of
starlight on a map; the knowledge of them, of where they
are in *this* world at any given time, as clear to her as land-
marks spotted from a helicopter flying high above an electri-
fied metropolis.

Bunny, for example, she can feel even now. So too their
mutual acquaintance Balam – presently sequestered, unless
Sunny is much mistaken, somewhere beneath the waterfalls
of San Ignacio.

But *this* one she can feel not at all. This so-called Gaius
Hemingway.

The creature bats away her question with one cloven
hand, airily dismissive. "You know how it is. Snap up a few
big-name companies, invest in a few charities and start-ups,
turn up to the right parties, and suddenly you're Rocke-
feller. None of the biographies you might have read came
from *me*, by the way – *I* prefer the enigmatic approach. It's
the fanboys who invent these horrendous hagiographies and
then spray them all over the internet. *Excruciatingly* embar-
rassing."

Sunny can only smile, faux-knowingly – her knowledge
of "Hemingway's" backstory extending no further until this
moment than those titbits Grady and Jonas have fed her.

"I confess myself confused by *your* role in this business,"
she says, "These friends of yours, these *Pragmatists* of whom
I've heard altogether too much for my tastes this evening:
they're no more than minor potentates with delusions of
grandeur, are they not? A regional flock of heirs-apparent,

grown cruel and self-important on inherited wealth and folie à deux. Not your usual crowd. And hardly exceptional in their vision – *or* its execution. Thus, I'm forced to ask: wherefore your interest? I find it impossible to believe you really are so *terribly* invested in the extension of human lifespan or the extrapolation of new toxins from some unplumbed fungal by-product."

Confused is perhaps an understatement. He'd always had a thirst for power, yes, and for manipulating others into exerting that power over their subjugates. But it was power enacted at scale, across orbits more expansive by far than those of the London aristocracy. His was the poison dropped into the ear of the emperor on the night before the battle; the sibilant voice beside the caliph at the feast, urging him on to ever-greater cruelties. The creature has lurked behind a chiliad of thrones, from Thebes to Toledo – the better in many cases to avoid the spatter of the blood that spilled upon them in the wake of his arrival.

Isolated experiments on the old and weak and vulnerable, whipping a sounder of none-too-bright princelings – and acolytes like Grady – into a semi-intellectualised brutality... they were such *small* acts, by his usual standards. So small, and so uncharacteristically *petty*.

"I have my reasons," he tells her, a note of pique entering the smooth bass-baritone. "Just as I'm sure you had yours in... where was it? Tikal? Nineveh?"

She's moderately taken aback that he recalls her time in *either* kingdom. *She* certainly has no memory of *him* from those periods – though she was, she will concede, rather busier back then, when her every day was gauzed in gold and crimson worship. When it seemed a god's work was never done, nor her appetites ever quite sated.

"Both," she replies, with appropriate hauteur.

"Both, then. My point being: ours is not to meddle in one another's affairs, and we need neither justify nor explain ourselves to one another. We do as we wish, *when* we wish, owing one another nothing. Unless something radical has changed in the order of things since last we spoke?"

Only me, thinks Sunny, the truth of the statement assailing her with the might of a bowman's arrow. *Only me and this fledgling conscience I'm struggling to shed.*

"You won't tell me?" she persists. "Not even so that you might satisfy an old friend's curiosity?"

"We were never friends." The voice is cold now, the face impassive stone. Before, the creature's demeanour suggests, he was prepared to entertain her questions, to tolerate her trespass into his domain. Perhaps it even amused him to do so. But his patience for such things is nearing its end. "I'm surprised you thought otherwise. And your curiosity and its satisfaction are your own concerns, not mine. I have... other things to be getting on with."

He looks rather pointedly behind her, at his sleeping human hostage – whose breaths, Sunny notes with alarm, have grown more shallow and more irregular in the minutes since she and "Hemingway" began their exchange.

How long do they have, she wonders, before the poison does its work?

And what *is* it, moreover, that this creature won't tell her? Why would he seek to do *any* of this in the first place? To what possible, inaudible drumbeat is he marching?

"I shall leave you to whatever you must do, in that case," she says, as lightly as is possible under the circumstances. "Take the girl, and be on my way."

He moves not a micron. "*That's* why you're here, is it? For *this*?" He gestures at the child with a clawed and slate-grey digit. "What an odd choice. I can't begin to imagine your motivations."

She shrugs, the tension thrumming through her sinews undermining any impression of nonchalance she might have hoped to convey. *"We need neither justify nor explain ourselves to one another* – you said that, did you not? But yes, the child is why I find myself here, in this... thieves' hole? Prison cell? Whatever one wishes to call it. And as I say: she and I will now be on our way, forthwith."

"No." He adjusts his stance, dense thighs widening into a Spaghetti Western posture intended, she must assume, to intimidate her into acquiescence. She'd be apt to find it amusing, were it not so enormously inconvenient. "Leave, by all means. I'd invite you to do so. But the girl stays. She isn't yours to take."

"Nor yours to keep." Sunny feels her hands begin to twitch – the urge to lash out at him, to beat him down and extract the child by force as he lies incapacitated an almost unbearably physical sensation. She could, she's sure, inflict damage enough on him to do so, even on this, his own turf: old though he is, she is older, and undoubtedly more cunning, if not always wise in judgement. And she is stronger; of this, she is confident. *Her* great age, unlike that of the fragile hominids among whom she walks, has brought only ever-compounding gains in speed and brawn and vigour.

Besides which, she has always disliked him, reckoning him smug and excessively calculating even by the standards of their species. Hammering a hoof into his sternum, delivering a donkey-kick to his groin or a knee to the softer reaches of his belly... any one of these, she hazards, would prove satisfying.

But as ever: there are rules. Rules older than them both,

older perhaps than the sum of their ages. Rules that govern their conduct toward one another, and all others of their kind: as stringent and as categorical as those that prohibit them from *directly* harming humans. Rules of which she would run afoul, should she strike out at him with tooth or limb.

There would be consequences. So very many consequences.

"What's to be gained by keeping her?" she asks, subtly adjusting her own stance in response to his. She will *not* be intimidated, and most assuredly not by a creature such as he. "Your secret club and its exploits are no longer quite so secret as they were. Your man Grady is captured and unburdening himself of what he knows even as we speak. How else could I have been aware of *this* place? The cat is out of the bag – it's a matter of days, perhaps even hours before the sordid details of your dealings enter the public domain, and I'd wager that not everyone will be so willing as your well-bred gulls believe to sweep the allegations under the carpet. The paqūdus will come calling at their doors, and soon, and whatever scheme you've been concocting will be over, or a hair's breadth from it. So why *not* release the child?"

"Because she belongs to me." He smiles. It is utterly maddening. "And now, also – because *you* seem to want her. And I rather like the idea of denying you."

She can't hurt him, she reminds herself. She is *forbidden* from hurting him. He knows it, too: thence his pomposity, his mafioso browbeating.

Nor, though, can she leave without the child. What, after all, would *Jonas* say, were she to do so?

You fail to understand that there are rules, she might tell the boy. *And the repercussions for disregarding them are significant. More significant than you can imagine.*

She sees the look on the boy's face as he takes in her excuses: the sadness and the disappointment. The sense that he believed her *better than that*, but has been proven wrong.

And, concluding that perhaps some rules deserve to be flouted even where there will be penalties to pay and pounds of flesh extracted, she launches herself forward. Drives a chiselled toe into the space between the former Gaius Hemingway's eyes, scoops the girl into her arms, and – as the wounded creature falls to the earth, clutching his face and cursing her name – hurls herself and her passenger up with an inhuman velocity through the open hatch in the ceiling.

———

THE FIRST UNATTENDED car she spots on the pavement outside, she steals: a brown Fiat 500, muted as a cardboard box. Bundles the bleeding girl into the passenger seat and conveys them both, with manic energy, to the accident and emergency department of a nearby hospital she's known, in one incarnation or another, for almost three centuries.

She leaves the girl by the entrance, slumped and very obviously unconscious in the gap between the automatic doors: secure in the knowledge that someone soon will notice her, and intervene accordingly.

Then she changes, once again. Adopts the falcon form of earlier that evening, and – very deliberately *not* thinking about the act she committed at the garage and its likely consequences – traverses the darkened sky to Denmark Hill and the home-turned-prison house of Leo Grady.

Where a fresh bloodbath awaits her.

"He ran into my knife," Jonas tells her as she surveys Grady's sanguineous corpse, now lying supine on the gore-stained tiles of the kitchen – innards exposed by the ragged wound at its gut, and dead eyes staring into nothingness.

The boy is still shaking, tremors racing along the skin of his reddened hands.

"He ran into his knife *ten times*," the ghost of Sean Keane adds, and sniggers.

Jonas winces. "It's not fucking funny."

Sunny has no time at present for the Bob Fosse songbook. "We'll need to move him," she says, her thoughts shifting to the practical tasks before them: the disposal of what remains of Leo Grady, and the inescapable clean-up thereafter. "Or rather, *remove* him. I suggest a potassium hydroxide solution – the cartels call it a pozole, I believe. Then a crushing device of some kind for whatever bones survive the liquefaction. There's a whirlpool Jacuzzi in my guest bathroom that ought to do the trick."

She'd been reluctant, before this evening, to disclose the existence of said hot tub to Jonas, lest he and Dan decide to avail themselves of its pleasures in her absence. It may be, however, that she need worry no longer about *that* possibility. Especially if Jonas himself pours on the lye.

To his credit, the boy is less fazed than he might once have been by her suggestion – though this will not, of course, be the first time the two of them have worked together to bury the evidence of an inopportune cadaver.

"What about the rest of this?" he asks, indicating the blood and ichor, the fallen knife.

"We clean it. All of it; every surface. And anything else you might have touched, these latter hours."

"And me?" The ghost of Sean Keane indicates the refrigerator that has been, of a fashion, his final resting place. "You gonna get rid of me as well?"

She contemplates this. "No," she tells him eventually. "I'm tempted in fact to recommend we relocate you somewhere more conspicuous – somewhere not easily missed, should anyone feel inclined to place an anonymous call to Scotland Yard sometime in the future. Perhaps to report the development of an unusual smell in the vicinity of the property, since the owner's disappearance."

She glances meaningfully at Jonas, who raises an equally meaningful eyebrow in response. "I think it's all online now," he tells her, as one might explain to an elderly relative that the Bakelite wireless no longer picks up the Home Service. "You don't have to call anyone."

There is silence as the three of them digest the proposal, and Sunny's mind wanders again – to Bunny, of all people.

Gentle, unexpectedly devious Bunny, who knows as well as Sunny the likely retribution Sunny has brought down upon herself.

Bunny, who might yet be the only one willing to help Sunny formulate a plan of action, were some suitably worthwhile proffer to be made in exchange.

A visit to the Midgrove Players from John Drayton, to name but one.

"And what about the rest of them?" the ghost boy says. "The murdering bastards at that club – the *Pragmatists*, or whatever. Are we doing something about *them*, or are they just gonna get away with everything, like they said they would?"

No, Sunny thinks. No, they are not.

There is *justice* to consider, and *fairness*, and yet other of those weighty abstract nouns of which Jonas is so fond. *Public safety. The prevention of harm.*

But more than this, there is the satisfaction that comes of petty retribution. And if she has indeed sown the wind and reaped the whirlwind, she can at the very least ensure the acolytes of "Gaius Hemingway" confront the consequences of *their* actions, too.

"Leave it with me," she says, the beginnings of a new idea already forming. "I daresay I'll think of something."

TWENTY-FOUR

PIERS

It was quite a trek through the woods to get to the lodge. Leaves and fir cones everywhere, sticking to his shoes – Piers felt like he was back at school, learning campcraft on a CCF weekender.

Bit different though, obviously. There'd been no girls up in the Brecons, for one thing. No gak allowed in the rucksack either.

It had been a bloody long drive to Gloucestershire, crammed into the back of Jasper's 4x4 and two of the boys there with him, one on either side. Piers' thighs were still giving him trouble from when his legs had seized up on the motorway.

Worth it, though. He needed a break, after that awful business with little Grady and the stuff they'd found in his kitchen. *Southwark House of Horrors*, the papers were calling it, like Grady was this year's Dennis Nielsen. Chopped up hands and feet in sandwich bags in the back of the freezer and a bloody *human head* starting to rot on the countertop.

Thank God the little man had done a vanishing act

before the law tracked him down, that was all Piers could say. Not that Piers thought Grady would spill his guts about the work they'd been doing, even if he *did* get caught. Or that anyone would believe him, if he did. But still: nice to know it wasn't something Piers or the rest of the boys needed to worry about. Yet, anyway.

Shame old Gaius had disappeared on them, too. Nobody had seen hide or hair of him since... well, since the House of Horrors had made itself known. He wasn't answering texts or emails, wasn't picking up his phone – even to Charlie. He hadn't checked in at any of the offices he used as bases, either. Not London, not San Francisco, not Amsterdam.

He was just... gone.

And a real bloody shame that was, in Piers' opinion. He was starting to like the old man.

It was Charlie's idea for them all to come out here. He'd gone ahead and rented a place out in the Forest of Dean, he said: nothing too grand, but big enough to sleep the inner circle, plus any girls or other entertainment they might want to order in. Somewhere that'd get them out of the city for a minute so they could take a breath and get their heads together.

Not a bad idea, Piers had thought. Not a bad idea at all.

All of them had made it up there in the end: everyone who'd been invited, half a dozen Jags and L460s pulling up outside a lovely little country house with woods and lakes all over, and no other buildings in sight. Perfect place to spend the weekend, really.

Charlie had been there already, waiting for them. Though a bit under the weather, was Piers' first impression when Chuck-Chuck had come out to greet them; his voice creaking and croaking, making the old man sound like a nuisance caller coughing into a hanky. Piers was pretty taken aback when he suggested they go out for a walk to the shooting lodge in the forest – *he'd* have stayed in by the fire with a Lemsip, in Chuck's position. But it felt a bit rude to say no, when the old man had shelled out for the place and would be splurging even more later on the girls and the ching. So out they trooped, Chuck leading the way.

And here they were, in the middle of a bloody forest, feet slipping on leaf-mulch and not so much as a smoking chimney to be seen above the tree-tops.

"We nearly there yet?" he asked Charlie. Old man hadn't said a word since they left the house – bit unusual, for him. Perhaps he was saving his voice.

"Almost," Chuck told him, in that same sex-pest croak.

A minute or two later, they reached the lodge. And pretty unimpressive it was too, in Piers' opinion: nothing but a run-down shack in a clearing, the kind of place a fairy tale witch might go to boil up kids in a cauldron. It bloody stank as well, a sort of silage-and-manure aura hovering in the air around it.

Charlie didn't seem to mind, though. The old man strode up to the door and yanked it right open, releasing a stronger waft of that awful smell into the woods. Piers gagged; couldn't stop himself.

"I'm afraid," Charlie said, turning around to look at them, "I haven't been altogether honest with you all. In fact, I would go so far as to say that I have actively deceived you. My apologies."

And that – that was *really* weird. He didn't sound a *bit* like Charlie when he spoke that time.

Something moved inside the lodge – a bloody *big* something, if the thud of its footsteps was anything to go by.

And then it shuffled out through the open doorway, and Piers saw it. Saw what it was: a pig.

Except... no – not a pig. A *hog*. A monster-hog the size of an ox, nothing but tusks and teeth and hair.

It was... chewing on something. Chomping, its mammoth's jaws crunching down on whatever was in its mouth. And Jesus Christ, was that *blood* in its whiskers?

It made a beeline for Charlie, its movements as slow and lumbering as a dinosaur's, though Piers got the sense that it *could* move fast, if it wanted to.

Charlie stuck a hand out towards it, like he was trying to shield himself from the tusks – as if a *hand* could do that, could protect anyone from something that size.

And the hog... the hog leaned into his hand and nuzzled it. *Nuzzled* it, softly as a bloody spaniel licking its owner's palm.

From somewhere behind Piers, there came a gasp: a muffled shout, and the crunching of twigs on rubber soles. One of the boys, trying to make it run for it.

"I shouldn't do that, if I were you," Charlie told them, addressing whichever of them it was. "The Beast is really rather speedy, for his build."

The crunching stopped, abruptly.

Charlie nodded, apparently happy with the outcome. And, even as Piers watched him, old Chuck... *shifted*: the lines of his body blurring and distorting, like playback gone bad on an old VHS tape, until Charlie's face, Charlie's chest and legs and arms were gone, obliterated, and a three-eyed giant with neon-blue skin and devil's feet and the sort of antlers you'd expect to find on an elk or a stag was staring back at them, grinning to itself.

"Charlie can't be with us today," it said, still petting the monster at its side. "Though I daresay he'd send his regrets, were he able. In better news, however: *we're* here, you and I and our rather pungent porcine friend. And he has, I must tell you, been building rather an appetite since his earlier hors d'oeuvre. Which brings us to what we might call the *real* question of the hour. That is: which one of you gentlemen would like to go next?"

AFTERWORD

Thank you so much for reading.

Reviews mean the world to small publishers like mine - so if you've enjoyed this story, we'd love it if you'd take the time to visit Goodreads or Amazon and tell other readers how you feel.

All the best,
T.C.

ABOUT TC PARKER

TC Parker is a writer and researcher based in Leicestershire, where she lives with her partner and family.

The author of the El Gardener crime trilogy (*The Debt, The Push* and *The Remembrance,* recently reissued as *The Long Con* omnibus) and the horror novels *Saltblood, A Press of Feathers, Salvation Spring* and *Hummingbird,* she's been a copywriter, a lecturer and, very briefly, an academic. Now she runs a semiotics and cultural insight agency by day and dreams up stories at night, when the kids are asleep.

Visit her online at www.tcparkerwrites.com

ALSO BY TC PARKER

Horror & SF/F

Saltblood

Salvation Spring

Hummingbird

A Press of Feathers

————

Crime & Thriller

To Coventry: A Hummingbird Murder Mystery

The Long Con: An El Gardener Omnibus

The Debt

The Push

The Remembrance

ABOUT NEFARIOUS BAT PRESS

Nefarious Bat Press is a female-owned independent publisher specialising in queer horror, crime and dark fiction.

Find them online at www.nefariousbatpress.com

TO COVENTRY

And she shall have murder wherever she goes...

The young men of Coventry are dying, violently and bloodily, and nobody seems to know why. There's no obvious reason for their deaths, and no connection at all between the victims.

Enter Sunny: demonic, immortal and bored to distraction by her new life in London. She needs a new challenge - another reason to get up from her fainting couch and grab the world by the throat. And the Coventry murders might be just what she's looking for. A chance for her to channel her inner sleuth, dust off her fedora and, if she's lucky - gather the suspects together for a shattering final denouement...

A pitch-dark comic-fantasy murder mystery with a light touch and a lot of anger, To Coventry takes the Hummingbird story in an unexpected direction - and brings a whole new meaning to some very old nursery rhymes...

"TO COVENTRY is an immensely enjoyable return to the universe of HUMMINGBIRD, one of my favorite books of 2022. Expertly woven elements of fantasy, horror, and social commentary all crafted in a delightful style that's simultaneously reminiscent of Terry Pratchett and completely unique, TO COVENTRY was a joy to read. Can't wait to return to this world again. Recommended for fans of Neil Gaiman, Terry Pratchett, and fans of wicked good writing in general"

- Laurel Hightower, author of BELOW and EVERY WOMAN KNOWS THIS

"A loving homage to the detective tale, with Parker's style elevating the form to something entirely unique"

- Coy Hall, author of A SEANCE FOR WICKED KING DEATH and THE PROMISE OF PLAGUE WOLVES

"A skilfully-written, compulsive story, and I can't wait for more"

- Kev Harrison, author of THE BALANCE, BELOW and SHADOW OF THE HIDDEN

HUMMINGBIRD

There's a storm brewing in Gallow: angry parents, protests at the school, a new priest up at the church with some very clear ideas on sin... and an unfamiliar face in the cottage on the edges of the village, carving sculptures out of skin and bone.

It's a powder keg. Even before the protestors start disappearing...

Jodie doesn't want trouble - just to be left alone to raise her son in peace.

Tanya wants more God and less wickedness in her own son's studies.

Tara wants to leave her complicated past behind her, if only it would let her go.

And all Jonas wants is to get some work done - and if he can make peace with his father while he's at it, then so much the better.

But the woman in the cottage and the priest up at the church - they have very different goals in mind. And Jodie and Tanya, Tara and Jonas... they're about to get caught in the crossfire.

***With a Foreword by Stephanie Ellis, author of* PAUSED *and* THE FIVE TURNS OF THE WHEEL**

"Hummingbird is the kind of novel labyrinth where the unexpected lurks around every corner. Parker's mosaic holds layer upon layer of gripping characters and supernatural tricks in a Pulp Fiction-esque horror show, where a monster's only weakness is another kind of monster. Immediately engrossing." -- ***Hailey Piper, Bram Stoker-Award winning author of* QUEEN OF TEETH *and* THE WORM AND HIS KINGS**